# THE DAY OF DISASTER

# THE DEPARTMENT Z SERIES

# THE DAY OF DISASTER
## DEPARTMENT Z

JOHN CREASEY

OPEN ROAD
INTEGRATED MEDIA
NEW YORK

ISBN: 978-1-5040-9183-1

This edition published in 2024 by Open Road Integrated Media, Inc.
180 Maiden Lane
New York, NY 10038
www.openroadmedia.com

# THE DAY OF DISASTER

# 1

## THE FUGITIVE

He was a youth, no more than twenty, but the fear of death was in his eyes.

He crouched in a ditch at the side of the road, grateful for the inky darkness as the convoy roared and rumbled past. The ditch was clammy from recent rain; the April night bitterly cold. The only light came from the dimmed headlamps of motor-cyclists weaving in and out of the heavier vehicles; demons of light and speed whom the fugitive feared, that night, beyond all things.

The youth had been in England before, but only in time of peace. Since then, he had learned the bitter way, how differently a stranger was received by a country and people swept by breath of war. Crouching there in his hiding-place as the ground quaked and trembled beneath the wheels and tractors of the machines of violence, he re-lived a night impossible to forget. A night when the men in the machines had been clad in field-grey, and the roadside and the hedges had been littered with the dead and dying.

A part of the British army was on manoeuvres, but this he

did not know, unable to associate this unceasing roar with anything other than murder and pillage and the cursing of the wounded. Lying there he heard those sounds again, throbbing through his mind, his heart, his very being.

There came a time when no tanks or lorries or motorcycles passed him. As their noise faded slowly into an unknown distance he dared to stand up, gasping as cramp shot through his limbs, causing him to fall helplessly over the lip of the ditch. He straightened up slowly, the agonising contraction of his muscles giving way to the lesser pain of cold and hunger.

He was obsessed, his mental vision distorted by privation and hardship.

He had spent two months in Belgium and another in France representing himself as a refugee from Alsace, and thus gaining sympathy, and enough food and drink to get him to the coast. In a small motor-boat with three Frenchmen he had set out for England, but a Messerschmitt had sighted them. The boat had been riddled with bullets, overturned and sunk.

He alone had survived, and with the help of a lifebelt drifted towards the English coast. Exhausted and unconscious, he had been thrown ashore. Coming slowly to life again, he had found himself repeating one name, monotonously, incessantly.

*Loftus.*

He had heard it from the lips of a man dying in a fever, and he remembered the other words, which made sense only in phrases.

'Loftus. Spell it backwards. S-u-t-f-o-l. Spell it backwards. See you through. Tell him anything you know. See you through. Loftus.'

The man who had uttered these words had befriended the fugitive. A burly, gruff-voiced socialist-Frenchman, he had behaved like most of his countrymen, cursing the Nazis and blessing the English, careful not to be overheard.

Then it had been said that this Frenchman was a spy.

He had been shot at and wounded by the Germans, and the fugitive had helped him get away. Beyond recovery he had lapsed into feverish rambling, muttering of England, always England. Then suddenly, in startlingly clear tones, the dying man had cried:

'Loftus. Spell it backwards.'

When it had seemed that he was on the point of death, a letter for him had reached Emile, since there were ways in which letters could be delivered without passing through German hands.

The spy, if spy he was, had read the letter, then fallen back, staring towards the sky.

'Emile—dare I trust you? This letter—get it to England, to—'

A warning had been brought, then, by a child from the town; the Germans were searching for Communists in the woods and the fields; Emile and his friend must be quite silent until the searching was over. It had lasted most of the day, dark field-grey uniforms had been close by very often. A dozen times the dying man had started to mutter, and Emile had thrust a hand across his mouth until the urgent danger had gone. When at last he had died, Emile had left him, not knowing whether his words had been a solemn trust to be honoured, or the outcome of delirium. More than anything else he remembered: 'Loftus. Spell it backwards.'

There had followed the journey across France and the Channel, until the moment when he had awakened on the sandy beach of an English cove. Later he had been able to find a gap in the barbed wire which ran along the coast, and reach the safety of the wooded land nearby, remaining hidden until nightfall.

He wanted to find Loftus.

He did not know where Loftus lived, nor how he could discover it. His mind would not let him face the difficulties, the virtual impossibilities; he was driven on by the obsession to find Loftus, doggedly determined to avoid capture.

He did not hear the movements on either side of the hedge.

He did not see the figures until they sprang upon him, crowding his vision with rifles, vague shapes of bodies, the white blur of faces. He uttered a shriek which carried itself into the bitter wind. A gruff voice said:

'Hold the blighter.'

'Stop it, you ruddy fool.'

He struck out wildly but weakly, while hands gripped him. The gruff voice spoke again: 'He's shivering like hell!'

A torch shone on his face, half-blinding him.

'Why, he's only a kid.'

'Kid or not, don't let him go,' said the first speaker.

'But who the blazes would have thought we'd been searching all day for this brat!'

The exchange passed over Emile's head. He tried to find words of English but he could not, until suddenly he shouted in a high-pitched voice:

'Loftus, Loftus! Spell it backwards, spell it backwards!'

'He's trying to be funny,' opined the man with the gruff voice.

'He's not,' said the other sharply. 'He's all in. Let's get to Teddy's place, if we get him warm we might learn something. All right, old chap, we're not going to knock your head off even if you are a ruddy Hun.'

They were friendly; that forced itself through the barrier of fear in Emile's mind. They were kindly, they did not hurt him, they talked of getting him warm. He stared at their vague shapes, barely discernible against the lowering sky; and then he pitched forward. He would have fallen but for their restraining hold, and he had no knowledge of being lifted over a man's shoulder and carried along the road towards a cottage not far from the Dorset coast.

Bill Loftus was learning to walk.

It was no easy matter, although after four months in bed, he had grown used to the idea that a man in the middle thirties who, until the fight in a Southampton hotel, had been more active than most, would have to learn to walk again.[1]

During the convalescence, after the amputation of his leg, he had experienced spells of acute depression. There had been brighter intervals, however, helped by his many friends and by the normal optimism of his nature, and when he had first started to use the aluminium leg he had found it amusing as often as not. When it no longer made him laugh it made him angry; getting angry with his own leg eventually amused him again. On the whole it was not a gloomy convalescence.

He was in a nursing-home in Surrey.

'Nursing-home' was the word used for it, although in fact it was a rather beautiful house reserved for the personnel of Department Z exclusively, and was run by Bob Kerr, himself handicapped by an artificial arm, and one of the earliest victims of the dangers of the Department's work.

Before losing his leg Loftus had been a vast man. He remained tall, two inches or more above six feet and five inches taller than Kerr, but his flesh had wasted. Now his lounge suite flapped about him in a wind which was warm even for April; it seemed to him that it slapped about his aluminium leg more than his flesh and bone one.

7

On the lawn which spread round the gracious Elizabethan house, in the shade of a gigantic Cedar, Loftus was standing quite still. Kerr stood ten feet away from him.

'Two to one you don't make it,' Kerr said. He was smiling; a rugged-faced, not particularly handsome man, very broad at the shoulders, and thick-set.

'Taken, in cigarettes,' said Loftus promptly. 'Packets of twenty.' He carried a stout stick in his right hand, raised it off the ground, and took a slow, careful step forward. He swayed; the stick went perilously close to the ground, but did not touch it. After balancing on both legs again he went forward more cautiously.

'We ought to set a time limit,' said Kerr.

'Shut up, you ass.' Loftus kept his mouth tightly closed, looked steadily ahead of him, and made two more steps. He was halfway to Kerr.

'Careful now, careful,' counselled Kerr. 'Bear a little to the left—I mean the right.' He stood unmoving, a hand ready to support Loftus if the latter failed at the last minute. Slowly, resolutely, Loftus advanced, until at last he gripped Kerr's shoulder with his free hand.

'That's forty cigarettes!' he said exuberantly. He drew a handkerchief from his breast pocket, and wiped his forehead. 'By George, for the first time in my life I really feel sorry for a toddler beginning to walk! Seriously, how did I do?'

'Within a week you'll be running,' said Kerr. 'I'm not sure that it isn't a record. Tubby Simm walked on his own after seven days, but he only had metal below the knee.' Kerr took out a cigarette case. 'This goes off the forty,' he added, 'I can't afford to give 'em away as well as lose 'em. What about a drink?'

'I've been thinking of it,' said Loftus, as they moved slowly towards the house. Inside the porch he rested for a moment, then stepped cautiously on to the parquet flooring. 'I wish the girls were here,' Loftus added, a trifle wistfully. 'It calls for a celebration. What time will they be back?'

'They're catching the four o'clock bus,' said Kerr. 'Can't be back before five. We'll have lunch, and then a couple of hundred up,' he went on. 'I suppose—' he hesitated—'I suppose you'll want to get back to London as soon as you feel sure of yourself?'

'Ye—es,' said Loftus. He looked at Kerr keenly. 'Why don't you come up for a few weeks? Craigie could find you plenty to do.'

'It's an idea, and I've often hankered after it, but I've got used to being down here. I'm afraid of getting unsettled if I start real work again.' He was frowning as he led Loftus into the low-ceilinged dining-room.

Moving across to a sideboard he took out whisky and soda. Loftus accepted a glass in silence, his eyes shadowed. He knew what Kerr implied, and he wondered whether he, himself, would feel the same in a few years' time. What Kerr really meant, of course, was that the office work which was all Department Z could really offer would not be satisfying. What work Kerr did for Craigie, the Department's Chief, he did at the nursing-home; he had not said so in as many words, but Loftus knew that he felt less dependent on others that way. It was even more than that; it was a way of avoiding constant contact with the more active agents. There must be times when Kerr yearned after the days when he had been Craigie's leading agent.

Kerr said: 'Bill, it gets under my skin sometimes. I can fly a 'plane as well as the next man, and God knows I want to. There are one-armed men in operating squadrons. I—' he paused and then went on abruptly: 'I applied for a job with the

R.A.F. I was turned down, told I was doing more useful work. Useful!'

Loftus smiled ruefully.

'Aren't you? You've been a godsend to me, and I don't mean that tritely.' He took a drink. 'Bob, I've a feeling you've developed a Department complex. You've been looking after this place for years, but now the tempo of the war has increased. Last Autumn's Russian and Libyan campaigns made you feel like a million dollars, absolute seething because it seemed we weren't doing a damned thing.'

'The difference being that you were doing something,' Kerr amended.

'That's just it,' said Loftus. 'I was doing Department work. It's peculiar—' he paused, searching for the right words, 'it's peculiar because it's one of the few things where each agent can feel he is doing, individually, a constructive job of work. Once we've done that, nothing else is really satisfying.'

'If you're trying to say it's an outlet for individualism, you're right,' put in Kerr, 'but the same applies to fighter pilots, they're quite on their own.'

'Only in the air,' said Loftus. 'They're subject to control when they're at the base. The discipline's there, although it's not so obvious. But damn it, why are we talking like a brace of blimp philosophers? We want something to do, we know what we want, and we know we can't do it. I found myself thinking one day last week I wished I'd never heard of the Secret Service.' He smiled a little, his lips curving wryly. 'I've been out of it for six months, and even now the very words sound unreal. Secret Service? I don't believe in it!' He laughed shortly. 'This I suppose is the natural swing of the pendulum after the walking triumph. Bound to come. Anyhow, here's something to eat.' He heard a maid approaching, wheeling a dinner wagon. 'Every time I sit down to a meal I think it's time I stopped brooding and realised my luck.'

Kerr smiled. 'Shouldn't we all? But between you and me, I'd rather go on short rations and be abroad.'

'How many men have you had here for convalescence?' asked Loftus. 'In the past year, I mean.'

'About thirty,' said Kerr.

Loftus stood up carefully, and went to the table.

'All right, Bessie,' said Kerr, 'we'll serve ourselves.' He smiled, and the maid beamed back as she wheeled her trolley ahead of her, closing the door.

'I was going to say,' went on Loftus as Kerr served vegetables, 'that you've put thirty of our men back on the job, and with one or two exceptions, like me, they've started work again fairly quickly. It's a job absolutely worth doing. It's your person and individual effect on 'em that does it. Craigie knows it. I've always known it. Can't you get that into your head?'

Kerr shrugged. 'All the same I'd like to be at something more definite, more—hallo, what's that?'

He broke off at the sound of a sharp knock on the front door. Moving towards it, he saw a youth in postman's clothing holding out a single letter.

'Mornin', sir, this be overlooked like on the mornin' round.'

The letter changed hands and the youth touched his forehead and turned away. Kerr glanced at the envelope, which was addressed to Loftus, and went back to the dining-room.

Loftus said quietly:

'That's Craigie's writing.' He took it swiftly and opened it with a sharp, decisive movement. Kerr, watching him, knew from his manner how much he was depending on finding work again with Craigie. Kerr's pulse was beating fast with vicarious excitement.

Loftus read swiftly, his eyes beginning to shine. He looked up half-way through and said abruptly: 'This is for you as well as for me. I'll read it aloud.'

'I'll read it over your shoulder,' said Kerr, reaching his side quickly.

The letter was headed 'Whitehall, April 11th;' and was written in Craigie's small, neat writing.

*Dear Bill,*

*I haven't much time to do more than just run through the outlines of this, and I'll leave you to work out the approach to it. A young Frenchman—he might be Belgian, or he could be a German acting the part—was seen coming ashore near Lyme Regis one day last week. The Home Guard found him after about fifteen hours. He was in a state of exhaustion, and was taken to hospital. He's still there—in Weymouth—and I can't get down to see him myself.*

*Apparently he's physically on the mend, but mentally unbalanced—that's the word given to me; I don't know what it implies. At all events, he's been repeating your name, thus 'Loftus, spell it backwards'. The last three words speak for themselves; obviously he's been in contact with one of our men.*

*You and Bob had better go and see him. He's fit enough, I'm told, for removal to the nursing-home, and you can keep him under your eye there. I don't know a thing more than I've told you, except that the only name he gives himself is Emile.*

*If you can't do anything about it yet, let me know quickly, and I'll try to get to Weymouth. One way and the other I'm so busy I want to avoid it if I can.*

*How's the leg? Christine tells me you're doing wonders with it already.*

There were the initials 'G.C.' at the foot of the letter, but even before reading the last paragraph Kerr and Loftus were looking at each other eagerly.

Loftus said: 'How long will it take us to get to Weymouth?'

'About three hours,' said Kerr. 'I'll tell Barney to bring a car round. I'd better drive, we won't want anyone else with us. And you'd better scrawl a note for the girls and tell them we'll be late. Bessie can get a room ready.' He hurried out.

All interest in food gone, Loftus stood up. He hardly noticed, as he went into the morning-room to write the note, that it was the first time he had walked unthinkingly on his new left leg.

1. Read *Go Away, Death,* by John Creasey.

## 2
# LOFTUS SINGS

L oftus sang.

He started when the Bentley, which Kerr nurtured as carefully as a hen protecting her chicks, was some ten miles from the nursing-home. Until then the journey had been silent, for neither man felt talkative, and neither was by nature inclined to talk for the sake of it.

But presently Loftus's lips had begun to curve at the corners, as if he saw a joke too precious to share. Then he begun to hum. Gradually he put snatches of words into his humming. Finally he raised his voice and threw his head back.

Kerr shot him a quick, sideways glance.

'For the first time since you've been up I wish you were in bed with the door shut,' he said pointedly.

'Liar,' rejoined Loftus. He was half-way through a second, slightly more Rabelaisian verse when Kerr joined in.

To the roar of their voices, the Bentley sped on, through Salisbury, through Shaftesbury, into the open country again.

All at once they noticed half-a-dozen military vehicles

ahead of them, small parties of infantry in full battle-dress on either side of the road.

'It looks like manoeuvres,' Kerr said.

'Keep your hand on the horn,' Loftus implored.

'Who's driving?' demanded Kerr.

'All right, all right,' said Loftus, 'have it your own way.'

It took them four hours to reach Weymouth.

They passed another, smaller convoy of men and war machines on the move, just outside the seaport, not knowing that the very men they passed had sent terror into Emile's heart six days before.

The hospital was in a residential quarter of the town.

A nurse, a sister, and finally the matron saw them. The first two were firm; the visitors could not see the patient Emile. The matron, a tall well-built woman with a face set in lines of severity which the expression in her eyes belied, received them in a small but well-kept office.

'I haven't given general instructions that you are to be admitted to the boy's ward, Mr. Loftus,' she said. 'I had a telephone message asking me to give you every facility, but not to allow it to be widely known.' If she felt curious about such a message, she concealed her curiosity well. She went on: 'He's been asleep for the past two hours, but I've just been told that he's awake again.'

Loftus lingered, sensing that more was to come.

'He's saying the same words—they're practically all he's uttered since he came round. "Loftus—spell it backwards".' The woman played with a pencil, not looking at either of the two men.

Loftus smiled; until then his expression, like Kerr's, had been almost wooden. Nothing in his face suggested a man of unusual intelligence, but the smile was transforming. It made him at once likeable and authoritative.

'That must be puzzling you plenty,' he said. 'How many people have heard him?'

'Five or six. Myself, Sister Ewan, two nurses and Dr. Shapgold.'

'I wonder if you could find out whether any of them have made the phrase a subject of conversation?' Loftus asked. 'If it has got about it doesn't much matter, but if it could be prevented it might be of service.'

'I don't think any of them will have talked,' said the matron, tentatively. 'I can't be sure, of course.' She looked a little disturbed. 'I'll do what I can to make sure that it isn't made a gossip item, Mr. Loftus.'

'Thanks very much,' said Loftus warmly. 'And if you could find out while I'm here whether it has gone the rounds I'd be very appreciative. Now—' he settled back in his chair, giving the impression that he had all the time in the world to spare— 'I wonder if you will give me a précis of your own, and the doctor's opinion of Emile?'

'Of course,' said the matron.

In five minutes, Loftus and Kerr knew that Emile was a lad of nineteen or twenty, under-nourished and, sometime within the past year or eighteen months, the victim of a flogging. He had two scars on his right leg, probably from bullet wounds. In his delirium he spoke a fluent, bastard French, interlaced with a number of Flemish and half-Flemish words. He had at one time been of good physique, and was probably of farming or peasant stock. Despite privations, he was in fair bodily health and would quickly regain lost weight. Mentally he was an enigma.

The matron went on slowly: 'I've discussed the case with Dr. Shapgold, Mr. Loftus. We agree that the way in which we might get over his present mental halt is to confront him with

the man whose name he is repeating so frequently, but—'
she paused.

'There might be difficulty in convincing him that I am the
man,' said Loftus slowly. 'Yes, I can see that. Has he shown any
liking for any particular nurse?'

'Yes, Nurse Caroll.'

'I wonder if Nurse Caroll could be in the room when I
speak to him?' asked Loftus. 'It's obviously going to be a heck
of a job to get him to talk. She's quite reliable, I hope?'

'I wish I had twenty others as good. She isn't on duty at the
moment, but I think she's in her room.' The matron lifted a
telephone. Nurse Caroll was in her room and would report
for duty, in five minutes. Loftus smiled his thanks.

'You're being a great help, Matron.'

'If you have in mind what I think you have,' said the
matron enigmatically, 'you are going to be a great nuisance,
Mr. Loftus.' She smiled. 'No, don't press me to explain just
now!' She relaxed a little. 'I hope you can help the lad.'

'I think we can,' said Loftus, and to Kerr's discomfort spent
several minutes explaining Kerr's activities at the 'nursing-home'.

As he spoke, there was a tap at the door.

'Ah, Nurse Caroll.'

Kerr rose quickly, while Loftus eased himself up with the
help of his stick.

It was not hard to imagine why the matron wished she had
twenty nurses like this girl. It was easy to see that she would
inspire confidence in her patients, and that she would find no
trouble too great to help them. She was beautiful all right, but
Loftus and Kerr were mainly aware of the intensity of her
eyes. They were blue, large and wide-set, the lashes framing
them as dark as her hair and her eyebrows. It was the curiously direct expression, however, that compelled attention.

Loftus thought: By George, she's lovely!

The matron introduced them, smiling, then turned authoritatively to Nurse Caroll.

'Mr. Loftus is going to try to convince Emile that he is his friend. I want you to go with him to the ward.'

'I see.' The girl's voice was quiet and a little husky. There was breeding in it, and in her face and figure. Again Loftus found himself curious about her, but he put the thought aside, as he commented easily:

'It probably isn't going to be a walk-over, and I hope you'll be able to help.'

'I wonder if I can go in the ward for a few minutes on my own?' asked Nurse Caroll quickly. 'I might be able to make him understand who's coming.'

'That's a good idea,' said Loftus.

The girl looked at the matron, received a nod of approval, half-turned, and then turned again and regarded Loftus steadily. There was an odd silence in the room.

'You are his Loftus, aren't you?' she asked.

'I think I can guarantee that,' said Loftus quietly. 'But he doesn't know me, except by name.'

'That doesn't matter. I just felt—'

She broke off and hurried out of the room. The matron was smiling as she lifted a telephone and asked for tea and biscuits for three to be sent to the office.

'Nurse Caroll has spent a lot of time with Emile,' she said. 'Her off-duty time as well as duty. I think she's a little afraid of what might happen if he's disappointed.'

'We won't disappoint him,' Loftus said.

'No—o.' The matron appeared to understand, or at least acquiesce, in the delicacy of the situation, chatting tactfully, and not too directly, about her staff as they waited for the tea. Nurse Caroll, it appeared, was one of three who spoke French, though the only one to speak it fluently. She had worked in London during the blitz, and during that time her only brother had been reported missing, believed killed.

'What was her brother in?' asked Kerr. 'Not the Southshires?'

'I think that's the regiment,' said the Matron.

'Oh,' said Kerr.

'Did you know the brother?' asked Loftus quickly.

'I know his wife's people,' said Kerr.

They were interrupted by the arrival of tea, which they had just finished when a message came from Emile's ward; could Mr. Loftus come at once?

Another nurse was waiting to guide him. She walked too quickly for him, then, looking round to see the cause of his delay, realisation struck her suddenly. She blushed a vivid red, her distress and solicitude almost harder for Loftus to bear than her youthful haste.

He smiled understandingly as he reached the ward, influenced at once by the hushed atmosphere of the room.

Nurse Caroll was sitting on the foot of Emile's bed, one of the lad's hands in hers.

'Here he is, Emile,' she said in French. 'I've promised to find him for you, and here he is.'

Loftus stepped slowly towards the bed, feeling the fast beating of his heart. He saw a face that was clearly young, and yet had lines at eyes and mouth which were more rightly those of one old enough to have experienced the bitterness of life. The eyes were grey, and deeply frightened. Had the youth not been so thin he might have been good-looking. His lips were trembling just then, and very pale. He looked at Loftus yet appeared to be shrinking away, as if afraid of him.

'This is Mr. Loftus,' Nurse Caroll said.

Loftus said in French almost as good as hers: 'I expect

Emile will know me better if we spell it backwards, don't you? S-u-t-f-o-l.'

One hand stretched out towards Loftus, the other still gripped the nurse's. The boy's whole body began to shake.

'Loftus, spell it backwards!' he cried. 'I have found him, found him!' He clasped warm, bony fingers about Loftus's hand, and the pressure was surprisingly fierce. 'The letter,' he shouted, 'the letter, it is for you, the letter!'

'I was hoping you would have a message for me,' said Loftus easily, and glanced at the nurse. He saw her shake her head, almost imperceptibly, and knew that she was telling him there had been no letter found on Emile. He had a queer spasm of acute disappointment, coupled with a conviction that for the moment at least he must pretend to know all about it, and not disappoint the invalid.

'The letter!' exclaimed Emile. 'M'sieu, for safety I place it in my boot. And now I have no boot, I have none!' His voice went upwards on a note of terror, rising higher and higher.

# 3
# FIND THE LETTER

Nurse Caroll released the lad's hand from Loftus's arm and held it, together with his other hand. She spoke quietly but with a stern, almost a sharp note.

'Your boots are downstairs, Emile. Don't behave like a child, or I shall lose my patience.'

Emile turned his gaze from Loftus quickly, and his trembling increased rather than eased.

'Mam'selle, please, I am sorry. Forgive.' He stared into the blue, almost disconcerting eyes, and something of her strength and calmness passed from her to him. He sank back on the pillows, steadier, calmer. 'The letter, please, get it for Mr. Loftus.'

'I'll go downstairs and get it myself,' Loftus assured him. 'What was it like, Emile?'

'It was—a letter.'

'Did you read it?'

'Many, many times, M'sieu. But it made no sense.'

'It was in English, perhaps,' said Loftus.

'But non, M'sieu, English I can read although with much labour. It was not in any language.'

'Then it was in code?' said Loftus insistently. His heart was beating as fast as his mind was working. Craigie had been right to send him here without loss of time. He had no serious doubt that the message in the letter had reached Emile through a Department Z agent in France. Craigie had known such a contact, of course, for it was a regular thing that when contacting with one another by telephone, and wanting to prove the genuineness of the contact, Department Z agents gave their name and then spelt it backwards. The simplicity of the system had ensured its safety; it had not been mis-used during the ten years since Craigie had inaugurated it.

Emile leaned forward again, less tensely.

'That is so, M'sieu. Letters and figures, all mixed up, so that they made nonsense. He read it quickly, M'sieu, very quickly.'

'Did he?' Loftus knew that to ask quick, direct questions would be to do more harm than good. The story had to come as Emile felt he could tell it.

'Yes, M'sieu, and he was so near to death. He had been wounded M'sieu, by the Boche, they had discovered that he was English, not the son of France that he pretended. Even I, Emile, did not know, for he came amongst us many years ago, and it was believed he came from Brittany. They are farmers, the Bretons! Often my father has talked of M'sieu Legarde, how foolish he was to talk of politics, for my father knew how the Boche worked in France, and knew that even before the war it was not safe for a man to talk too freely.'

'Your father is a wise man,' Loftus said.

Emile stared at him, the large staring eyes suddenly filling with tears. He did not speak for several seconds, and when he did his voice was choked and his lips were trembling violently.

'He—is dead, M'sieu. He was killed by the accursed Boche,

he would not surrender English wounded.' The young voice gathered speed, the words seemed to come from every fibre in the thin body. 'My mother, she watched them kill him, they held her and made her watch while the bullets struck him. And then they mistreated her, mistreated her!' His voice rose to a scream, his eyes were glazed, and he was looking into horrible things, into unfathomable distances of the mind. The nurse stood up, but retained her grip on the lad's hands. Emile cried:

'And afterwards she killed herself, my mother, my beautiful mother, she killed herself. Dead, dead, dead, all dead,' he muttered. He sank back, his eyes closed, his body heaving.

Nurse Caroll said: 'It might help him, now that he's talked about it.' She released Emile's hands and eased him downwards in the bed, then stepped to a table and brought a damp, cold cloth to sponge the lad's forehead. 'You won't try to make him talk any more, will you?'

'No, not now,' Loftus hesitated, and then said spontaneously: 'Nurse, if the patient has to be moved, will you come with him?'

'To where?'

'A private nursing-home,' said Loftus.

'I doubt whether the matron will release me,' said Nurse Caroll quietly.

'It can be arranged, if you'll say "yes".'

'Yes,' said Nurse Caroll. 'Will you go now, please?'

Loftus went out, closing the door gently behind him. Back in the matron's office he said apologetically: 'I'm going to be the nuisance you expected, Matron.'

Kerr looked puzzled, but the matron lifted her hands in a gesture of resignation.

'I thought so,' she said.

'What is this?' demanded Kerr.

'Matron made it pretty clear that she thought we'd want to take Emile away, and that to give Emile the best break he can have we'd need Nurse Caroll. So—' Loftus, half-laughing looked across at her.

'Maddeningly selfish of you,' Matron answered decidedly, then laughed a little. 'Oh, well, I needn't be professional with either of you, that's a help. When do you want to take him away?'

'It had better be tomorrow morning,' Loftus said. He explained briefly what had happened, and then added: 'So we must have his boots.'

'I'll send for them.' The matron telephoned for Emile's clothes, then listened for a moment before saying sharply. 'Are you quite sure?...' She replaced the receiver looking at Loftus worriedly. 'What a strange thing. He didn't have any boots when he came here,' she said. 'His feet were bare.'

There was less than half an hour of daylight left of that warm Spring day, and the evening was growing chilly when Loftus and Kerr stepped into the Bentley.

The matron had promised that the patient and Nurse Caroll would be ready at ten o'clock in the morning; Kerr had undertaken to send an ambulance for them. Not once had Loftus been compelled to use pressure. In bidding them farewell, the matron asked them not to keep the nurse longer than they needed her, and hoped they found the letter.

She evinced no curiosity about it at all.

Kerr let in the clutch, and as the car started off he said reflectively: 'A fine woman that, Bill.'

'Ye—es. Both of 'em, for that matter.' Loftus paused. 'I hope to God we find that letter. Did you ever meet Tim Langham?'

Kerr shook his head.

'Hm. I saw him once before the war when he slipped over for a week-end to tell us that the Nazis in the Calais district pretty well outnumbered the anti-Nazis. Craigie sent the report through, but I expect it was filed with a thousand others.' Loftus was frowning and staring ahead of him. 'Langham's name in Lens was Legarde. The information we had from him up to six months ago, when I went out of the limelight, was always right up to the mark. That letter matters a whale of a lot.'

'Well,' said Kerr, 'if the police haven't got his boots, the Home Guard will have. They won't have been thrown away.'

'I hope not,' said Loftus.

He followed the directions the matron had given him, and Kerr pulled up outside the main police station a few minutes after leaving the hospital. Loftus showed a card which was signed by the Home Secretary, and gained him a quick entry into the Station-Superintendent's office. A tall, thin-faced man appeared to understand that they did not want to waste time. He telephoned two or three people and then replaced the receiver with a gesture of annoyance.

'None of our men took the boots,' he said. 'You'll have to see the Home Guard people. They passed him on to us on Wednesday night. You've got a car?'

'Yes,' said Loftus, 'but—'

'You'll want a man to take you round, now that it's nearly dark,' said the Superintendent. 'I'll lend you one.' He telephoned again, and replaced the receiver. 'Detective Welton knows the country well, and if you have a long job you'll be all right with him.'

Loftus thanked him, and they went downstairs.

They found a plainclothes man waiting with an expression of great eagerness beside the car.

Once more settled in the Bentley, Loftus stretched his legs as far as they would go. The artificial one was aching, or it appeared to be, far more than the other. His thigh was certainly painful; there was no imagination about that. A picture of Emile and of the nurse passed through his mind. He went through the disjointed conversation he had held with Emile, and he felt the poignancy of the shouted statement, reading into the high-pitched voice something of the horrors of the German occupation.

Then he found himself thinking of Nurse Caroll, and smiled a little grimly.

When the car stopped he said: 'You get out, Bob, will you? I don't feel like moving.'

'Of course,' Kerr said. He moved off with the policeman to the Platoon Commander's office, going through for the third time the rigmarole of asking for Emile's boot.

Five minutes later he returned to the Bentley; by then it was quite dark. Loftus leaned towards the window.

'Any luck?'

'They don't know anything about them here,' said Kerr, 'but the patrol which found him is somewhere in the country—Welton knows where to get hold of the men.'

'Good,' said Loftus.

He was not feeling good. The aching in his thigh was worrying, while the continued failure of the boots to appear was strangely reminiscent of some nightmarish fairy-tale. Legarde, alias Langham, had sent a message through Emile; the fact that Langham had given away that simple 'spell it backwards' code to a French youth was evidence enough that Langham knew the message to be of vital importance, and one which must be sent through at all costs. Loftus wondered why he, himself, had been so casual about it until then, so blind to the urgency of it.

He saw it now all right. He was obsessed with the need for finding the letter, was on tenterhooks lest the boots had been destroyed or lost. He tried once or twice to tell himself that he was getting worked up unnecessarily, but knew that was not true. In him there had grown a conviction that this thing mattered, that it was indeed an affair of urgent importance.

It was as if a sixth sense lurked in him, warning him of what was to come, of the issues which depended on the discovery of the letter. That was the first stage; without it he could do nothing, and it was vital to do a great deal.

As the car went through the narrow country roads, the two masked headlights giving a fair light, he found himself perspiring although the night was cold. Suddenly the figures of men showed in the beams of light, and Loftus saw a barrier half-way across the road. He cursed it, surmising it would prove to be an inspection of registration cards, and another delay when delay was intolerable. He stopped himself from snapping at the uniformed man who spoke through the open window.

'I'd like to see your registration card, sir, please.'

Loftus had it ready. Apparently they were to make a detour, since operations on the main road were in progress, and would last for some hours.

Kerr said: 'We haven't time to waste.' He spoke shortly.

'I'm sorry, sir,' began the Home Guard, but the policeman said quietly: 'We're on police business, and it's urgent. If you can't let us through, bring an officer.' This, however, was not easily done, and when the Home Guard Captain finally arrived he was annoyed.

'In the middle of exercises we've been planning for a month!' he exclaimed irritably. He examined the police warrant, and seemed prepared to submit, although reluctantly. 'Who do you want to see?'

'The patrol who found a Frenchman near here last week,' said Kerr.

'Oh, I remember. Let me think, now—Bott and Anderson brought the man in—'

'Do you know where he was first taken?' interpolated Loftus.

'No, you'll have to see them. They're at Hern. But as you're in a hurry you'd better go straight through. I'll send a man with you.'

A Home Guard clambered in beside them. Without him they would have been stopped half a dozen times, and several times they were challenged. Loftus felt impatience growing within him, and yet logic told him that this thing was neces- sary, that it was good to know that the Home Guard was so thorough in its training.

They passed the scene of operations at last, and then the car gathered speed. Finally the headlights shone on a wayside cottage.

'I think this is a Home Guard post,' said Welton. 'I'll slip out and see.' He hurried along the narrow path. Kerr was muttering something under his breath.

'What's that?' asked Loftus.

'I was saying they've probably given them away for a rummage sale,' said Kerr. 'Of all the lousy delays this is the lousiest. Why didn't you show your card? They wouldn't have been so awkward if you had.'

Loftus said slowly: 'I don't know that it's wise to let 'em know just how important it is.'

'Oh,' said Kerr, a little blankly, 'Why not?'

'Call it a hunch,' said Loftus. 'I'm worried about those boots. I want to know why they weren't sent to the police, if not to the hospital.'

Kerr said: 'You're not thinking they might have been kept back deliberately?'

'I'm thinking it's possible,' said Loftus. He did not speak of his fears again, although across his mind there had flashed the possibility that Emile had been followed to England, or discovered in England by people who did not want his message to get through.

On the surface the idea was fantastic. He did not know how Emile had made the journey, but if he had been followed the second man would surely have been caught by the Home Guard patrols. He remembered then that he had very few details of how Emile had been found; at the time they had not seemed necessary. Now he wished he had obtained every item of information possible.

He looked up to see Welton returning.

'I don't know whether you would like to see the old lady, sir. She says the kid was brought here, and she took off his boots because one of his legs was bleeding. But—'

'Go on,' said Loftus quickly.

'She says the boots were stolen, sir.'

'Stolen!' snapped Loftus. 'Open the door for me, will you.' He would have climbed down too swiftly had Kerr not been out of the car by then, standing by to lend a hand. The trio walked up the narrow path, and were admitted to the tiny parlour of the cottage. There were photographs and pictures on all the walls, while bric-à-brac lay everywhere, even to white china spaniels on the floor.

'Be keerful, now, be keerful!' a high-pitched voice admonished from the gloom. 'Mind me dogs, if you please, m'boy gi' em to me when he stayed in Margit.' A very old woman with a lined, nut-cracker face stood protectively before the dogs.

Loftus drew a deep breath; he was not in the mood for being tactful, but it would be folly, now, to rush developments.

'I'm sorry, ma'am,' he said.

'Well, what is it ye want, worrying an old woman at this

time o' night? Me boy's out on duty, an' his wife's in village, doing some flummery wi' nursing at the Red Cross.'

'Your son's in the Home Guard?' asked Loftus.

'Aye, an' a better soldier than any.'

'I'm sure of that,' said Loftus. 'He brought a fugitive here last Wednesday, you say?'

'His friends did,' snapped the old woman waspishly, 'my Teddy would've knowed better. But I did all I could for the boy, an' no one can say other!'

'I'm sure,' repeated Loftus stonily. 'But we want to find his boots.'

'Boots!' She spat the word. 'Wore right out, they were, and not worth anyone's taking, but they went from the rubbish heap at the back, an' any man's a liar who said they didn't. Cheap, worthless things they were, not worth anyone's trouble.'

'Oh!' said Loftus. He felt a sudden wave of relief, although he had no real reason for it. 'You're sure they weren't worth anything?'

'I wouldn't gi' ye sixpence at a jumble sale!'

'That's odd,' said Loftus, lying deliberately. 'The man says they were a new pair.'

The woman raised her voice to one of near-frenzy.

'He's a liar, then. Green you be if you believe a Frenchie. Put 'em on th' waste heap I did, and—'

Loftus said: 'And you took them off again. They were good boots. If you didn't sell them, who did you give them to?'

There was a moment of silence; and then the high-pitched voice sank to a whining note of injury. She had not thought, she sniffed, anyone would mind. She'd given them to Teddy. The coupons, that was the trouble, it wasn't the money it was the coupons. Waste not want not, gov'ment dinned in from morn till night-fall. Blame them.

'That's enough,' said Loftus sharply. 'Where are they?'

'Teddy's got 'em on,' said the woman with another sniff. 'He won't like having to gi' them up, mister, and that's a fac'.' The little eyes grew sharp.

'Where's your son?' demanded Loftus.

'On dooty, up at spinney.'

'Come on,' said Loftus to Welton. 'Do you know where the spinney is?'

'Let Welton go and fetch the man,' suggested Kerr. 'We can wait for him here.'

'If ye'd like a cup of tea,' began the old woman.

Loftus said: 'That's an idea.'

The woman shuffled out with Kerr, who saw Welton off, their voices loud in the silence.

Back in the room Kerr said thoughtfully: 'So you were worried about those boots?'

Loftus grinned in relief.

'You could call it that.'

Kerr, took out his cigarette case. 'You even had me wondering. They shouldn't be long—there goes the car.'

'It'll be midnight before we're back home,' said Loftus, 'but when I've got the letter I can 'phone Craigie. It's an odd show. It's got under my skin.'

'And mine,' said Kerr.

They lapsed into silence as the sound of the Bentley's engine faded into the distance. Another car passed almost immediately, but they thought nothing of it; they would have thought more, had they known the driver wanted Emile's boots as urgently as they did.

4

# URGENT ERRAND

The man in the second car had received a telephone
order a little more than an hour before. It had been
brief and to the point: he was to follow the two men who were
looking for Emile's boots, and get the boots.

Put like that, it sounded easy.

The driver had no doubt of its difficulty, however, and as
he drove he was not only cold and worried, but desperate; he
had to obey the order, for refusal would bring about personal
disaster. He had been threatened with that several times, and
knew what it was like to imagine a firing-squad in front of
him, to hear the officer's final word of command. He could
almost hear the crash of shots, and feel the pain as the bullets
entered his chest.

He hated pain, although he lived by it. That was why he
had first taken a bribe for a trivial piece of information, long
before the war had started. Others had followed, until the
money was accompanied by orders, not requests.

He shied from the word 'spy'.

He convinced himself that no information he gave away

was important, that it did not cost lives or money or material, that he was only passing information which a hundred others had probably obtained. It was the only way he could ease his conscience, although there were times like this, when he knew that he was lying to himself and felt the shame of it.

But he went on; failure meant disclosure, and he could not face that.

He had told the man on the telephone many small things. The name of the regiment stationed at such-and-such a village or town, their approximate numbers, their apparent amount of equipment. He had talked of the cargo ships waiting in south coast harbours, given names and number of British ships that he could see. He had passed on information about the aeroplanes hidden at certain aerodromes in the south-west, where he lived and worked.

All this information was easy for him to come across.

Finding the boots was another matter. Only once before had he been given such a task, and then he had carried an automatic in his pocket, knowing that if things went badly he must use it if he was to escape. The telephone-man had assured him that if ever he was forced into difficulties he would be given prompt and efficient help. He believed it, not from any reasonable conviction, but because he wanted to, refusing to admit even a chance that he might be found out and put on trial.

He had stopped some distance behind the Bentley, having managed to pass the Home Guards with even less delay than Loftus and the others.

He was within earshot of Detective Welton when the latter had come out of the cottage, and had overheard most of the instructions. He was thus able to follow Welton fairly easily. Knowing the country, he had no fear that he would lose his quarry. He stopped his car when the Bentley stopped, and hurried along on foot to the spinney. There was light from the headlamps of the parked Bentley.

It showed a game-keeper's hut, and outside it three men. Welton was one; the others were in Home Guard uniform. The man with the automatic drew close enough to hear the old woman's son cursing the newcomer. At first he flatly refused to take off the boots, but Welton was persuasive, and presently 'Teddy' gave way. 'Oh, all right, 'ave the ruddy boots. 'Oo the 'ell wants 'em, anyway.' He began to untie the laces while Welton tactfully placed another pair beside him.

The man with the automatic drew within ten yards. He was trembling, and his hand was clammy about the steel of his gun. He knew that if he were to get the boots from the three men he must shoot, or convince them that he proposed to do so; and he was not sure that he could carry such a bluff through.

He moved another yard forward, and then he felt a hand on his shoulder. His lips opened but the cry he was about to utter was stillborn, for a hand covered his mouth.

A voice whispered: 'Stay where you are Brice. When both boots are off, let them know you're here. Tell them to put their hands up.'

The man out of the night knew him; he was a friend. Brice's throat was dry and rasping. He swallowed painfully as the man left him. A shadowy figure moved to the right; he thought he saw another, to his left.

He focussed his eyes on the trio by the game-keeper's hut. Teddy had removed the other boot, and Welton was stooping down to pick them both up. Teddy was still muttering oaths when Brice forced himself to go forward. He would not have succeeded but for the knowledge of the man or men watching him.

His voice, when it came, was pitched several notes too high.

'Put your hands up!' He stepped just inside the beam of light, his automatic pointing towards Welton. He saw the way the two Home Guards stared at him, gaping in their surprise. He saw Welton stiffen. 'Put them up! Put them up I tell you!'

They ignored him, hardly thinking he could be serious.

The two Home Guards, Teddy without his boots, leapt at the same time, and he squeezed the trigger of the automatic, blindly. He saw Teddy fall forward, as the gun was sent flying from his hand.

Brice crashed backwards.

Welton stood quite still, holding the boots. The whole thing had happened so quickly that he had not time to think. But he realised that Teddy had been hurt, and he began to move forward, uttering a sharp exclamation as he did so.

Then he saw the other two men.

They were converging on him from the right and the left, no more than vague, distorted shapes, as yet. He saw the gun in one man's hand, caught in the shaft from the masked headlamps. He did not know whether the other was armed, but he did know that they wanted the boots; there could be no other explanation.

He began to run.

He heard the sneeze of a bullet from a silenced automatic as it missed him, the thump as it buried itself in the trunk of a nearby tree. He heard another shot, and felt a red-hot pain in his left leg. It made him stagger but did not stop him altogether.

He heard a cursing, milling group not far behind him; but he had only one pursuer. The man fired again and Welton felt a sharp tug at the boots in his hand. There were many trees and saplings, and he was by then in darkness, beyond the range of the light. He thought, with a gasp of relief, that he could get through safely, until he saw the flash of flame from another shot near him, and a second in front of him.

There was someone there too.

He stood quite still, then turned to the right. He could hear footsteps following him and knew that more than two men were in his wake; the spinney seemed alive with them. He knew then that he could not get away safely, but that he might be able to dispose of the boots.

He was in a comparatively clear patch; and he did the only thing he could. He hurled one boot and then the other high above the close scrub into the over-hanging trees. He did not see them soaring upwards, but he heard them crashing through the branches.

He heard another shot, and plunged face downwards, he saw a torch light shine about him, and then gasped as a man kicked him heavily in the ribs.

'Where are they?' The voice was rough, but it was an Englishman's.

Welton said nothing, feigning unconsciousness.

'I'll kick your ruddy ribs in. Where are they?'

Welton kept quite still, until a boot crashed into his ribs with such sickening force that he heard the bones crack. He gasped: 'Away. I threw them away.'

He heard an oath, and as yet another blow fell agonisingly on him, he lost consciousness. He did not know that the second Home Guard had managed to crawl away after being wounded, and was staggering along the side of the road, just alert enough to know he must throw himself into the ditch if he heard a car behind him.

\* \* \*

Loftus, looking at his wrist-watch, compared it with the clock on the mantelshelf, and frowned. In front of him, and between him and Kerr, was a small table on which was a wedge of fruit cake, a teapot and two empty cups and saucers.

The teapot was cold.

'One hour and five minutes,' Loftus said sharply. 'I don't like it, Bob.'

'You're too jittery,' Kerr said lazily. He was smoking a pipe, both looking and feeling more content than he had been for a long time. 'No one else knows about those boots, old man, you're working yourself up over nothing.'

'I may be,' Loftus admitted without conviction. 'But even so, I don't like it, and if I had two sound legs I'd be on the way to that spinney. What about it?'

Kerr stared at him. 'Seriously?'

'Certainly. I hope I'm wrong, but I can't steady myself as I'd like to. Have a look round outside anyhow, will you?'

Loftus was worried as much by his inability to walk freely as by fears of what might be happening to Welton and the boots, and Kerr, sensing this, felt that it was necessary to ease the tall man's mind. 'I'll stroll towards the spinney if the old girl'll tell me the way.'

The old girl was only too glad to tell it to him.

Towards her Loftus felt a cold hostility, almost a hatred; for she had stolen Emile's boots, which had played so important a part in what might prove an epic of endurance.

Kerr was a long time.

Ten minutes passed, fifteen, and twenty. He stubbed his second cigarette, stood up, and went to the door; walking was not so easy as it had been, and he knew that he had tried himself too far. Yet the knowledge that he had done so was a comforting thing; it proved that he was not entirely out of

37

action. Moreover, Craigie had shown that he was still, in some degree, dependent on him.

Both things consoled him.

He opened the front door and walked stiffly down the path, but before he reached the gate he heard a call: 'Is that you, Bill?'

It was Kerr, from some distance off; and there was a note in Kerr's voice which alarmed Loftus. 'Get the old woman to have boiling water and bandages ready.' Kerr's voice continued eerily, 'and find out where the nearest telephone is.'

Loftus stood quite still for some seconds; then he turned abruptly to the cottage. His shout brought the old woman running, and he gave her orders swiftly, before joining her in the kitchen.

'Where's the nearest telephone?' Loftus hardly recognised his own voice. He was trying to reassure himself that his earlier fears had been groundless; but he could not.

'It'll be at the farm, sir.'

'How far's that?' Did he hear a sound at the gate, and footsteps? Or was it his imagination.

'About a mile, maybe.'

'Is there a bicycle here?'

'Well, yes. There's m' daughter's bike, but it'll be too small for you, sir.'

'Get it to the front door as soon as you can,' said Loftus. He no longer wondered whether there was a sound at the front; he knew there was. He went forward in time to see Kerr entering the front door carrying a man over his shoulder. Blood was seeping through his battledress.

Loftus said bleakly: 'What else?'

'God knows,' said Kerr. 'You were right. There was an attack on Welton. Three or four men at least, and shooting. What about that telephone?'

'There's a woman's cycle at the front door,' said Loftus, 'and the 'phone's at the farm we passed coming here. What are you going to do?'

''Phone for help,' said Kerr.

'Save time, and get to the Home Guard,' said Loftus, taking his wallet from his pocket. He showed the card signed not only by the Home Secretary but by high officials of the Army. 'We can use this now that the alarm's been raised. Get 'em busy.'

'Right.' Kerr hurried out, while Loftus bent over the wounded man. The old woman had sidled up, and was removing the battledress far more expertly than he could have done. She cut away shirt and vest and began to cleanse the wound. He thought bleakly that she had her good points; showing skill and aptitude for emergency nursing that was now to be of invaluable service to him.

He fetched and carried for her.

The time dragged, but a little more than half an hour later he heard the sound of approaching cars. Three passed the cottage, but one stopped outside it. Kerr came in, breathing heavily; he had cycled at more speed than he knew, and had not fully recovered, despite a five minutes' car ride back.

'Are you coming?' he said.

'Yes,' said Loftus. They went out together and entered a car driven by a Home Guard lieutenant. By the time they reached the spinney the other cars were already there, their headlamps converging on the spot of attack. A dozen men were moving in and out of the trees.

Kerr went on to investigate, and returned in ten minutes; two men with him were carrying Welton, on a stretcher. The old woman's son was coming with a second pair of stretcher bearers, while there was a third man waiting to be brought along.

Welton regained consciousness on the way to the hospital. He was not delirious but he was in great pain. Talking was an agony for him, but he forced himself to say to Loftus:

'I threw them—into—the trees. Oak trees—near the road.'

'Good man,' said Loftus gently. 'Good man, Welton.' He turned as easily as he could, and spoke to Kerr. 'There's still a chance,' he said. 'We'll have to wait until morning, but we can have the place under guard all the time. If the boots have lodged in the trees, or scrub, we'll find 'em.'

'Ye—es,' Kerr said slowly. 'What are we doing—staying here overnight?'

'Of course,' said Loftus. 'We'll ring Lois and tell her what's happening, and arrange for an ambulance to fetch Emile. And I'll give Craigie a ring. There isn't much doubt that this little affair is worth all the attention he can give it.'

Loftus fell silent, until the end of the journey. He used the telephone in the matron's office, sending word to Bob Kerr's Lois, and a message to Christine; Christine had yet to convince Loftus that she was in love with him.

He talked to Lois, rang off, and put the London call through. Then, while he was waiting, the door opened to admit Nurse Caroll.

Kerr stood up; Loftus sat near the telephone and looked at her, quite expressionless. He was reminding himself that she had known of the importance of the boots: Nurse Caroll and the matron, but none others to his knowledge.

5

# BACK FROM ADVENTURE

The nurse closed the door quietly. It occurred to Loftus
for no reason at all that he had not yet seen her smile.

'Good evening,' she said. 'May I have a word with you, Mr.
Loftus?'

'Of course.'

She nodded her thanks, her manner precise and imper-
sonal. 'Emile came round not long ago. He's very anxious to
make sure that you found the letter.'

'Ye—es, I suppose he would be,' said Loftus. He felt Kerr's
eyes on him, and wondered whether Kerr had any idea of
what was passing through his mind. He was thinking that it
was strange that Nurse Caroll should have learned of his
arrival at the hospital so soon, and that she should voice
curiosity about the letter. Under Emile's name, it could very
easily be her own.

'Will you see him?' the nurse went on.

'I can't immediately,' Loftus said, 'I'm waiting for a call
from London.'

'Can I take word to him?' asked the nurse.

41

Loftus hesitated. He wished that he did not need so long to make up his mind; before his crash he would have been much quicker off the mark.

'Well, yes,' he said at last. 'Will you tell him that we found the boots, and that the letter is on the way to London.'

'Thank you,' said Nurse Caroll.

There was nothing at all to indicate whether she was pleased or sorry. She turned away immediately, closing the door as quietly as she had done when she had first entered. Kerr took out his cigarette case, proffered it, and said, after a moment's pause.

'Now what's on your mind?'

'Did I make it as obvious as that?'

Kerr laughed. 'One learns to read the unwritten word, old boy. Was it really necessary to lie to her; and to Emile?'

'To Emile, anyhow,' said Loftus. 'Bob, what do you know of the Carolls?'

Kerr had been expecting the question; he spoke at once, giving Loftus the impression that he had prepared his answer beforehand. Loftus grew aware of the fact that he did not know Kerr really well, that he was apt to look on the ex-flier much as he would on the many agents of the Department who had worked with him for many years past. That was wrong. There had been a time when Kerr had been in Loftus's shoes, and virtually controlled operation. There was that extra something in his mind, just as there was in Loftus's, which enabled him to immerse himself in intelligence work, lifting him far above the average agent.

'Not a great deal,' Kerr said, 'except that her brother, Rex, was at Eton and Balliol about my time. He was older than this girl by seven or eight years, I should say. He married Anne Brandon, and I knew Anne fairly well. You're not asking yourself whether the nurse was the source of the leakage, are you?'

Loftus smiled with a certain relief.

'So you've got there too?' he said. 'Yes, I am asking that. Who else could there be, the matron apart?'

'Someone could have been listening-in.'

'Ye—es.'

'Or Emile could have talked in delirium to another nurse.'

'Ye—es,' repeated Loftus. 'It's possible, Bob, but I'm worried. Things aren't running as they should do. I wish we knew the whole story of Emile.' He ran a hand through his hair. 'But that's not the most important issue at the moment. I'm going to have some nasty minutes until we find those boots.'

'And if we don't?' asked Kerr.

'I'm not going to like it,' said Loftus, 'by heck, I'm not. But we needn't start jumping our fences too soon. I—ah, that'll be Craigie.'

He reached forward across the desk for the telephone as the bell rang, lifting the receiver eagerly to his ear. Kerr leaned back in his chair, smoking in silence.

At the other end of the wire, in a large office in Whitehall, Gordon Craigie heard Loftus's voice and looked towards an armchair at the far end of the room. The man sitting in it had his back to Craigie; the top of his head, showing above the chair, was covered with crisp, wavy brown hair. A spiral of smoke curled upwards from an invisible pipe.

Craigie, whom very few people beyond Department Z agents knew except as a civil servant who did some obscure work, spoke quietly.

'Yes, Bill, what's happening?'

'One way and the other I don't know,' said Loftus clearly, 'but getting down to the root of the matter it's not so good, old man. All ready?'

'Yes.' Craigie drew a pad towards him. 'Go ahead.'

He made notes in a shorthand which he had perfected himself, writing swiftly as Loftus talked. He knew that Loftus would give him only the essential details, but they increased with every second, as the lines round Craigie's mouth deepened. His grey eyes were half-closed as he wrote, and his thinning grey hair flopped forward over his forehead.

Loftus finished with: 'So I'm waiting here to see what the local people have to report. They may know who got the news from the hospital—as far as I can gather the dead man isn't a Home Guard, and had no particular business at the spinney. I think—' he paused, then added quickly: 'Hang on a minute.' Craigie waited, hearing a confused mutter of voices at the other end, and then Loftus spoke into the mouthpiece again, his voice a trifle more brusque. 'Still there, Gordon? ... good, the dead man's been identified. He's a Dr. Brice, a man with a small country practice somewhere near here, who does a little work at the hospital. I'm trying to find whether he was here this afternoon. Meanwhile will you see what you can find about the Caroll girl?'

'Leave it to me. Is that the lot?'

'Good lord, how much more do you want?'

Craigie smiled.

'As much as you can get! Just a minute, Bill. How are you feeling in yourself?'

'We—ell,' said Loftus slowly, 'giving a bit, and taking a bit, you might say I'm all right, and you can mark me up for duty forthwith.'

'Good. Where are you staying at Weymouth?'

'I haven't thought of that yet,' said Loftus. 'Supposing I leave a message at the police station? If you want to get in touch with me you can ask 'em for the number.'

'That'll do. Sleep well.'

Craigie replaced the receiver, smiling a little. For the

moment anxiety about the message in Emile's boot was less important than the knowledge that Loftus was well enough to be at work again, and that his activities would not be hampered as much as Craigie had feared. He had come to depend a great deal on Loftus.

But he knew that Loftus would have to be replaced as the active leading agent; and he looked reflectively at Bruce Hammond, from whose pipe smoke was rising so imperturbably, wondering if he, himself, were right in nominating him to be Loftus's successor.

Craigie, a man who habitually dressed in grey and cultivated a non-spectacular appearance, sank down, now, on the opposite side of the glowing fire.

On his left was a cupboard, the door of which was ajar owing to the fact that the contents were too crowded and untidy to enable it to close completely.

One end of the long room, that about the fireplace, might have been the apartment of a bachelor in any flat in London; the other was barely, even austerely furnished as an office.

Craigie looked at his companion, noting a lassitude that amounted almost to exhaustion.

He had seen him often enough before, although for several years the other had been in Germany or in parts of occupied Europe on Department Z work. Full, wide lips curved amusedly as Hammond regarded Craigie in return. 'Will I be all right for the job, sir?'

Craigie smiled.

'I'm trying to make sure,' he said. 'Do you feel able to cope with anything that comes along?'

'A tall order, but about the right height. Pity a month's sleep can't precede it. But I'll settle for one night's rest. What's the trouble?'

'I don't know, yet,' said Craigie. 'It's rather at the iceberg stage, four-fifths under cover. You knew that Loftus had been hurt?'

'He lost a leg, yes. Bad show.'

'I'd rather like you to take over what jobs he can't do for himself.'

'Oh!' Hammond's eyes held an eager expression that faded almost at once, as if he did not believe that the decision would really go in his favour. 'We—ell,' he said. 'I've been used to free-lancing on the continent so much that I mightn't be all that successful as a member of a team.'

'You'd be free-lancing here too,' said Craigie dryly. 'Loftus has been doing so for three years. The only difference is that you can be in constant contact with the office, instead of quite on your own. But if you'd rather stick to the old job, and get back to France at the end of the week, say the word.'

'Freddie can take over from me there,' Hammond said hastily.

Craigie chuckled.

'All right, Bruce, you'll do. Now—'

He plunged into the story of Loftus's search for Emile's boots, his meerschaum going cold in the telling. Bruce Hammond's pipe, however, continued to emit little spirals of smoke, while his expression settled down to one of contemplative and almost dreamy interest.

No Englishman working abroad for Department Z could fail to experience a full mede of excitement, of danger, of anxiety and disappointment. Hammond's life had been the more precarious because he had been Craigie's report-centre in France since the war had begun. He had the advantage of being able to speak French not only fluently, but like a native, and even during the days of the German occupation and after, he had continued to live in Paris, an apparent dilettante who dabbled in art and writing and who when the Germans had really started their comb-out of 'undesirables' had behaved in so exemplary a fashion as to have been safe from suspicion for the greater part of eighteen months.

Then they had discovered his true work.

Craigie knew that the full story of Hammond's journey across France, Spain and Portugal would never be told; Hammond had never talked much about himself, or those things which happened in the course of his work. He accepted his orders and obtained a surprising number of satisfactory results, but his reports never went beyond a bare statement of those results, and any discoveries he had made while getting them.

Craigie finished, and automatically reached for a tin of tobacco on a table by his side. 'What do you make of this, Bruce?'

'I should say it was fairly obvious,' said Hammond, stifling a yawn. The lids of his eyes were heavy with sleep, although that did not affect the alertness of his manner. A peculiar alertness showing even through his fatigue. 'Langham passed on written information to Emile. The Huns discovered it, but lost sight of the boy. Knowing that he'd probably try to deliver it to the English authorities, they alerted their contacts on this side of the Channel. They're pretty thorough, you know. Didn't you say that he'd been machine-gunned by a Messer-schmitt?'

'A boat-load of fugitives was gunned the day before he was seen coming ashore,' said Craigie, 'and there were bullet marks in his clothes.'

'Call that two and two,' said Hammond, 'and there's your four.'

'Quick going,' said Craigie.

'Oh, I don't know. A relentless working away at detail is practically automatic with them. If there's anything that's significant, it's the fact that they used four or five men in their attempt. The thought of those boots decorating an oak tree has its humours,' he added, and stifled another yawn. 'Will it be all right if I get down there tomorrow?'

Craigie nodded as he pressed a button beneath the mantelshelf. A sliding door opened, and the light from the office glinted along a stone passage and down a narrow flight of steps.

'Thanks,' Hammond said quietly. 'I'll put all I can into it. I might—' he hesitated, 'I might be able to get an idea or two about what Langham was doing. I know what he was working on three months ago. So long.' He raised a hand, turned and walked down the stairs.

Craigie closed the door, then stood looking into the fire for several minutes. He believed that Hammond had kept something back; he knew of no other agent who so deliberately refused to report partial information until he had gathered in and tied up the whole. Hammond had been right in saying that he might find it difficult to work in England after he had been his own master abroad.

Craigie shrugged, and went to his desk.

Bruce Hammond found his way through a labyrinth of sandbags outside the front door of the Whitehall building where Craigie had his office, and stood still for some seconds to accustom himself to the darkness. He heard the tramp of sentries walking up and down, and a mutter of conversation between an A.R.P. warden and a policeman. A taxi and several buses passed him but he preferred to walk to his Jermyn Street flat. The mystery of London in the black-out was all about him, blanketing the capital in a strange, unnatural anonymity.

Hammond strolled on, turning Craigie's story over in his mind. It was pleasing to think that Craigie believed he could fill Loftus's place; Loftus—whose name was legendary throughout the Department.

Loftus's grave injury was a bad show for them all. Yet he was not right out of action; somehow this courage to continue as a lesser influence was to be expected of him. He, Hammond, must be careful not to make it seem that he was usurping any of Loftus's authority—more, that was, than circumstances made absolutely necessary.

It was difficult to believe that Loftus would be hard to get on with; on the other hand, any man must feel a little sore at taking second place where he had once reigned so superbly.

Oh, well, said Hammond to himself, I'll be seeing him tomorrow, and we can size each other up. He whistled under his breath as he went down Haymarket, eventually reaching Jermyn Street a little under half an hour after leaving Craigie.

There was a strangeness in climbing the two flights of stairs to his flat, for he was so seldom in it. Taking the flat at all had been an extravagance, but a pleasant one. It pleased him to think that he had a pied-à-terre in the West End, that he could be free of hotels on the short spells he managed to get in London. Now, if things went as he hoped, it would be more or less a permanent home.

He let himself in with a key, then looked with regretful eye on an easy chair drawn up near an electric fire. He was too tired for a mere rest. All he wanted now was to get into bed quickly, and sleep for twelve hours. Then he would be able to look at the new problems with a clearer mind.

He was home, this was England; and there was at least a chance that he might stay here. He remembered, with a smile, when he had first joined Craigie's service, eight or nine years before, and his blinding ambition had been to go abroad and be domiciled in France.

Now he pushed open the bedroom door, but before he had

switched on the light the door sprang back. It startled him, making him aware that someone might be lurking in the flat, on the watch for him.

He waited before switching on the light.

It was absolutely dark, and silent. He held his breath, but could hear no sound of anyone breathing. With a sudden movement he pulled the light switch down, and stepped to one side; he would not have been surprised at some form of attack, but none developed.

'I'm getting jumpy,' he thought, and looked behind the door of the bedroom, to find what had prevented it from opening.

For a split second his mind and his limbs refused to work, as he stood staring at the body of a woman, a woman hanging from a hook at the top of the door.

6

# WHY HANG THE LADY?

I t was not a hallucination.

It was real, a body which drooped from a hook, a body about whose neck a cord was tied, pulling cruelly. It was of a woman, dressed conventionally enough, except that she wore no shoes or stockings. From the ankles her feet drooped downwards, white and small.

Faced with a tangible body, however gruesome, Hammond's tension relaxed and he stepped forward. Attempting to ease her weight from the cord, he saw that one shoulder of her coat had caught against a second hook, so that the full pressure had not been on her neck.

He unfastened the cord tied about the main hook, then carried her to the bed. She was quite motionless, but he had been wrong to think she was dead; he could see a faintly beating pulse in her throat, and another on her temple. He stared down at her, completely bewildered. This was his flat, no one else had any right to it; nevertheless, that right had, somehow or other, been usurped.

He wished he were not so tired. He went into the bath-

51

room and filled a bowl with cold water, then returned to the bedroom, and began to bathe her forehead.

He noticed that her hands were small and well-kept, her clothes of good quality. The only strange thing in her appearance was her lack of shoes and stockings. He searched the room for them, but found no trace. Baffled, he stopped by his whisky cabinet and poured out a stiff finger, then lowered the glass abruptly.

'What's the matter with me?' he asked abruptly. 'The ruddy stuff is probably doped.' He put the glass down and lifted the receiver of the telephone. He called Craigie, but had no answer. Frowning, he ran through the names of the men he knew in the Department, Davidson, Carruthers, Kerr—no, Kerr was with Loftus—the Errols.

Yes, the Errols.

He looked up their numbers in the directory, and dialled it. After a pause an easy, masculine voice answered him: 'Errol speaking.'

'Which one?' asked Hammond.

'Mark.'

'Oh,' said Hammond. 'Is Mike there?'

'Who is speaking?' The voice was still pleasant, but the casual note had gone.

'Hammond,' said Hammond, and then remembering that only to a few of the agents was his name known well enough to spring to mind immediately, added 'D-n-o-m—'

'Right! Where are you?'

Hammond gave his address, and added: 'Will both of you come round and oh, for the love of heaven, bring some whisky!'

Something like a chuckle sounded over the wire.

'Do I detect a note of desperation in the last plea? Anything brewing?'

'Nothing much,' said Hammond, and added as if to himself: 'All I want to know is—why hang the lady?'

'A lot of 'em deserve it,' said Mark, and rang off. Hammond lit a cigarette and went back to the bedroom. The girl was still unconscious, but she was breathing more easily. He wished he could understand the absence of stock-ings. He examined the soles of her feet, finding no trace of cuts or dirt; clearly the stockings had been taken off in the flat; unless, he thought, she had been brought by car and carried to his room.

Why his room, of all the places in London? And how had anyone obtained a key? He had been to great trouble to get a special lock made, and as far as he knew only he and Craigie held a key.

He found his mind clearing, his fatigue battened down as it had so often been in the past. He stepped to the window and pulled aside the curtains, making sure that there were no marks on the frame, and no suggestion that the window had been opened more than the few inches he had left before starting for Craigie's office earlier in the day. Then he went to the front door, looking for scratches; he saw none. There was no indication whatever that entry had been forced.

'Damn it,' he muttered, 'she didn't come down the chimney.' His pondering was interrupted by the voice of the girl. It quavered uncertainly from the direction of the bedroom.

'Who—is that?'

He stepped swiftly back. The girl had eased herself up on the pillows, and was staring round her.

Hammond said: 'Hallo, how are tricks?'

The girl said: 'Who on earth are you?'

'You wouldn't know, would you? By name, Hammond, Bruce. Bruce is the christian name. Who're you?'

She caught sight of her bare feet and jumped convulsively.

JOHN CREASEY

Hammond nodded. 'I felt puzzled by that, too.'

The girl looked up at him, apparently as bewildered as he. She put a hand to the bed cover, and rolled part of it between her fingers, dazedly. In a high-pitched voice, she said: 'This isn't my room!'

'Well, we've got something to start on,' said Hammond, 'We agree about that.'

'But how did I get here?'

'We both want to know that, too.' He put his head on one side and regarded her with a new interest. 'Do you feel all right?'

'Why shouldn't I?'

'Well,' said Hammond slowly, 'young ladies who wander into strange bedrooms and go to sleep on other people's beds might do it all as a matter of course, I suppose, but it doesn't seem to fit you. Usually—' he waved a hand in the air, 'they lose their memory, or sleep-walk.'

'I wish you'd stop talking drivel. Do you mind telling me what all this is about?'

'Mind! I'd love to, but—'

The girl put a hand to her neck, touching it gently. 'Will you explain why you brought me here?' There was an imperious note in her voice, and it was easy to believe that she was used to being obeyed.

It was strange that she seemed completely unaware of the fact that she had been found hanging behind his door, unconscious and probably not a long way from death. Unless she was acting very cleverly—a possibility he had to bear in mind—she had no idea of her narrow escape.

'How much longer are you going to stand there gaping?' she demanded sharply. 'I want to know what this means.'

'I can't blame you for that,' said Hammond, 'since it is a

54

state of mind in which I find myself even more firmly entrenched.'

She said: 'Are you trying to tell me that you didn't know I was here? That you don't know how I got here?'

'Not only trying, but doing so.'

'You actually expect me to believe nonsense like that?' she asked flatly. 'Where are my shoes?'

'Well,' he began tentatively, but she cut him short.

'If you've taken them to make sure I can't get away—'

Her words were cut through by a loud ring at the front door.

Hammond said abruptly: 'Can you walk?'

'Of course I can walk.' She stood up quickly, uttered a sharp exclamation, and sank back on the bed. For the first time she was frightened. 'What have you done to me? What are you looking at me like that for?'

'A small matter of precaution,' Hammond told her. 'I'm just making sure you don't try to go out by the window. I'll be back.' He went into the hall and opened the door, standing aside as Mike and Mark Errol entered, two large men who were very much alike. As the door closed they stood regarding him intently; it was another absurd episode in a night of absurdity, for in their expressions was an undoubted degree of suspicion.

Then Mike Errol smiled.

He was distinguishable from his cousin only because his hair was not quite so dark, for the rest they were astonishingly alike.

Mike put out a hand.

'Bruce, my son, I apologise.' He gripped Hammond's hand firmly, and from beneath his coat produced a bottle of whisky. 'Here we are.'

'Whisky and friends, in that order,' put in Mark Errol.

Hammond remembered then that it was their habit, when

55

together, to complement each other's sentences, to play the fool and to do all they could to confuse their companions into wondering which was Mike and which was Mark.

Now he said abruptly: 'Stop fooling, Mike. I can't take it just now—but one of you might pour me out a drink.' He did not want to ask them questions, to know why they had regarded him with some suspicion.

Mark uncapped the whisky, then stopped short.

'Hang it, you've a full decanter here!'

'It mightn't be safe to drink,' Hammond said.

Those words did more than anything else had done to make the Errols drop their flippant manner, to send the last rather puzzled gleam from Mike's eyes, and to make Mark say:

'Oh, that's the angle is it.' He poured the drink. Hammond swallowed it slowly. Then he said in a low-pitched voice: 'There's a girl in there. I know absolutely nothing about her, or how she got here. There may be a spree of some kind or other before the night's out, and I sent for you two because I'm so ruddy tired I can hardly keep my eyes open. I got back from Lisbon yesterday.'

Mike and Mark nodded.

They had come prepared to find that Hammond was not Hammond, and that the call had been a trick to get them to the flat. Since Emile had uttered the words: 'Loftus, spell it backwards,' Craigie had advised his agents that the identification code might be misused.

Had Loftus been there he could have told Hammond that the Errols were agents who could be relied on to the last degree in any emergency, that they only needed telling what had to be done, and if it were humanly possible, it would be done. A dozen times they had acted as excellent foils to Loftus; and unconsciously Hammond used them as foils then.

He led the way into the bedroom.

The girl was now sitting against the head-panel of the bed, her bare legs still uncovered. She stared at them without speaking; all three judged that she was frightened.

Hammond put a hand in his pocket and smiled. Either the Errols or the whisky had brightened him considerably, and he felt more in control of the situation.

'Friends of mine,' he said. 'Now seriously, we ought to get down to finding what you're doing here, and why.'

'Certainly—' began Mike.

'Not,' said Mark.

'Shut up,' said Hammond. 'Supposing we start with your name, Miss—'

She began to speak with a rush.

'I'm Hilary Crayshaw; if you do anything to me you'll regret it. My father will spend millions to make sure of that. Give me some shoes, let me get away from here. If you don't I'll start screaming. I'll yell for the police. Go away and leave me alone!' She paused for breath, and Hammond thought that although she was certainly nearer thirty than twenty, she had remained, predominantly, a spoilt child. She uttered her name, and coupled her father with it, as if that would prove the open sesame; and it was true that the name of Crayshaw did stand for something.

Anyone more hide-bound by convention would have admitted that it stood for a lot; the names of Crayshaw motor-cars were household words, as were Crayshaw aero-engines which were being fitted in an increasingly large number of bombers and fighters. Crayshaw's vast combine, devoted to motor-car engines in peace time, had been turned into one of the biggest engine suppliers to the British Forces.

'Hilary Crayshaw,' Hammond said, and smiled again. 'The name has its attractions. Now look here, Hilary, will you, can you, get it into your head that we don't mean any harm to you?'

'Then why am I here?'

'I just don't know,' said Hammond. He believed that the moment of crisis was over; she would prove amenable now. 'Would you like a cup of tea? Or something stronger?'

'I—tea,' she said. She touched her throat again, gingerly, as Mike and Mark Errol turned towards the kitchen, sensing that Hammond needed a few minutes on his own with the girl.

'They'll get it,' Hammond assured her. 'You won't feel like a cigarette for a while, then? D'you mind if I smoke?' He leaned against the foot-panel of the bed, smiling ruefully. 'It's taken us a while to get round to this,' he admitted 'but do you mind telling me what was the last thing you remember?'

'I was—' she hesitated. 'Where was I? Oh, yes, at the Lamplighter.'

'The Lamplighter?'

'That's what I said.' Her voice was tinged with impatience again, the slightly arrogant impatience of the spoilt. 'You can't know much about London if you don't know it, it's absolutely the latest place.'

'A nightclub?' Hammond said, almost wonderingly. 'I thought they'd died with the blitz.'

'Where have you been hiding yourself?' demanded Hilary. 'Of course they didn't. They were closed for a while, but there are dozens of them open now. What else can one do?'

'We—ell,' said Hammond, 'there are other things. War work for—'

'Oh, that's not for people like me,' said Hilary sharply. 'Father's money does a lot more than a hundred girls could do: that's quite enough for one family.'

'I see,' said Hammond, woodenly. He thought of the girls he had seen in France, of the horrors they were voluntarily enduring there and elsewhere in Europe. 'Anyhow, you were at the Lamplighter. Don't you remember anything else?'

'I was a bit giggly,' Hilary Crayshaw said. 'I'd been mixing 'em, and Ferdie got some absinthe from somewhere, it—' she stopped abruptly. 'Damn it, where's Ferdie?'

'Definitely a point,' said Hammond.

'He always sees me home if I'm tight,' said Hilary with a frown. 'I remember him helping me out of the dining-room and then—and then I think I passed right out.' She brushed a hand across her face, touching the groove round her neck. 'Where's a mirror?' She leaned forward, but Hammond deliberately stopped her.

'It's nothing, you just had a fall. It's clear now that you either passed out through mixing your drinks and taking too many of them, or you were drugged. In any case your Ferdie didn't look after you, and you were brought here. You're quite sure you don't remember anything else?'

'Of course I don't,' she said impatiently. She put a hand to her hair, and added: 'Where's my handbag? I must do something to my hair.' She did not add that there was a mirror in the handbag also, but Hammond smiled grimly to himself at the obvious subterfuge.

Then he frowned.

'I've searched the flat for your shoes. I would have found the handbag had it been here.'

He was looking at her all the time. He saw the expression freeze on her face, saw the shadows fill her eyes. She sat upright, staring at him.

'That's a lie! It's here, you've taken it, that's what you wanted!'

'Don't act like a spoiled brat!' snapped Hammond, 'I'm tired of it. The handbag's not here.'

'But it must be; I can't have lost it.' She forced herself to move away from the bed, took several faltering footsteps towards the dressing-table, but sank down on a chair before she reached it. Her eyes, wide open now, held real alarm.

She was looking desperately about the room.

'I can't have lost it,' she repeated in a low voice, 'I can't have done. Oh, my God, what will he say?"

'What will who say?' demanded Hammond sharply.

'Father.' She stopped looking about her and turned her face towards him. Her voice rose upwards to an hysterical pitch. 'Give it back; you've got to give it back!' When he did not speak she half-rose from her chair, sank down again and then with a great effort stood up and jumped towards him, striking out with small, clenched fists. 'Where is it, what have you done with it?'

She collapsed as he fended off her blows; falling face downwards.

Mike Errol pushed open the door.

'Now, now,' he said soothingly. 'Here's the tea. And look—'

'What we found,' put in Mark, just behind him.

'In the larder,' finished Mike, holding out a red leather handbag. 'Could this be Hilary's?'

# 7
# RED LEATHER HANDBAG

Hammond stared at the girl, and the girl stared at the handbag like one who was seeing undreamed-of terrors. Her manner made him feel not only puzzled but a little alarmed.

Mike went on as if there was nothing unusual in the situation.

'You must have been hungry,' he said, 'and put it down while ferreting. It is yours, I suppose?'

'Y—yes,' she said.

Slowly she took it from the tray, and unfastened the clasp. Lipstick, powder compact, hair-grips, a pencil, a handkerchief, a mesh purse, were upturned in an untidy heap.

Then she stopped.

'It's gone,' she said dully, 'it's gone.'

'It may be somewhere about,' said Hammond with an effort. 'If you'll tell us what it is—'

'I can't, I can't! What will he say?' It took no great effort of imagination to see that she was frightened of her father; from what Hammond remembered of Crayshaw, he was a man who inspired fright in a great number of people.

Mike put the tray down, and said practically: 'We may as well dispense tea now that it's made. Will you have a cup, Bruce?'

Bruce nodded; carefully Mike Errol filled four cups. Mark was looking at Hilary with puzzled eyes, while Hammond watched her hand shaking. She took a few painful gulps of tea, then pushed the cup away.

'Will you take me home, please? He'd better know.'

'What is it you've lost?' Hammond demanded.

'It doesn't matter,' she said lifelessly. 'It doesn't matter.'

Hammond looked at the Errols and judged from their expression that they were thinking it would probably be wise to do as the girl asked. He did not think it likely that she would be persuaded to exchange confidences, but he could at least learn if she were being watched.

His mind made up to that, Hammond rose quickly. 'Mike, will you come with me? If you'll stay here, Mark, in case anything else happens, it'll be useful.' He saw Mark Errol scowl, knowing that the suggestion would be unpopular, but he voiced no protest.

'What about her shoes?'

'I can carry her downstairs and into a cab,' said Hammond.

'We needn't bother about a cab, I've got our bus,' said Mike.

The girl said nothing, except to tell them when they asked her, that she lived in Audeley Street, Number 177a.

With a feeling of fantasy akin to that which he had felt when he had first seen her, Hammond carried her downstairs to the stationary car.

The drive took over ten minutes, then Mike turned in his seat.

'Shall I get the subject introduced?'

'Yes,' said Hammond. 'Give me a shout when it's all right to bring her in.'

He watched Mike fade into the darkness, waited until he heard a knock at the front door, a murmur of conversation, and then the closing of the door. He felt very lonely, for the darkness now seemed to be of greater density. The girl sat motionless, clutching her handbag. An occasional car passed the end of the road, and once he heard plodding footsteps.

For the rest there was only silence.

Then the door of the house opened again.

'All clear,' Mike called. 'Mind the step.'

Someone else spoke, and then the thin glimmer of a torch lit up the way.

Once in the hall, the light was good. Mike was standing by the side of a man of medium height, one who most of the people of England would have recognised, for Sir Noel Crayshaw had received as much publicity as his internal-combustion engines.

All Hammond really noticed about him was that he had a pointed beard and a well-trimmed moustache, and that his expression was grave.

'Hilary, my dear.' Crayshaw stepped forward, and the girl looked at him with lack-lustre eyes. Hammond had expected an outburst of excuses and explanations, but the girl only said:

'I've lost it. Someone took it.'

'My dear child!' Crayshaw's voice was deep and mellow. 'You really must not concern yourself about that now! Mr.—' he looked at Hammond, and Mike supplied Bruce's name, 'Mr. Hammond, can I presume on your good offices to carry her to her room? Her maid will look after her.'

Hammond nodded.

'Thank you. I will lead the way.' Crayshaw mounted the stairs ahead of them. There was an odd tenseness about his manner, despite his courtesy and his concern. He turned on the landing to see that Hammond was close behind him, nodded, reached the next landing, and then walked along a wide passage with curtained windows on one side and doors leading from the other.

One door was standing open; a maid, in cap and apron, was standing by a four-poster bed, the sheets of which were already turned down.

Hammond lowered the girl to the bed.

'Thank you,' said Crayshaw gravely. 'Now if you will come with me I will be able to express my thanks for your very kindly action.' He led the way downstairs, Hammond following. Although Crayshaw's back was towards him he felt as if the man's eyes were boring into his.

Mike was still in the hall.

The servant opened a door to the right of the hall, and then withdrew. Mike went first Hammond followed, and Crayshaw brought up the rear.

'I think, gentlemen,' said Crayshaw quickly, before either of them could speak, 'that I owe you an apology and an explanation. I think perhaps you will understand me when I tell you that my daughter has been a source of great anxiety to me, particularly in the past few years. There is an explanation—' he stepped to a cabinet, pressed a button, and stood back as the doors slid open to reveal an array of glasses, and several bottles. 'An explanation which only suffices in part, of course. Two years ago, Hilary's fiance was killed in a flying accident. Since then she has not been quite normal.'

He brought out a bottle of cognac.

'Not quite normal,' he repeated, while Hammond waited, fascinated and tongue-tied. 'Unfortunately she mixes with a rather worthless set, a habit only too popular with the young folk of today, especially when they have no need to worry about where their next allowance is coming from. I had thought her cured, but—'

He finished pouring, handed them a glass apiece, cupping his own with long, sensitive fingers.

'Now let us sit down, gentlemen.' He waited until they were seated, then continued in a sharper voice: 'She takes drugs, of course. Twice she has undergone a cure, but always there is the relapse. I have been told that in certain irresponsible moods she is suicidally inclined, and for that reason—have always made sure that she had a reliable escort. In fact I employ a man for just that purpose—one socially irreproachable you understand. Tonight, he failed me. Just why I cannot say.' Crayshaw stopped, sipped the brandy, and then said in a very abrupt voice: 'She tried to hang herself, didn't she?'

He looked at Mike, which gave Hammond the moment he needed to get over the statement—it was more than a question—and to shape his answer. Mike, because he did not know what had happened, returned a blank stare.

Hammond said: 'No, she didn't.'

Crayshaw turned abruptly, moving his whole body.

'Nonsense! The mark under the chin—'

'Mr. Crayshaw,' said Hammond quietly. 'Do I have to remind you that it was I who brought your daughter here safely tonight?'

Crayshaw, snapped: 'The evidence is quite unmistakable.'

'It certainly is, but not of what you suggest. That she was nearly hanged is true enough—but she did not hang herself. The circumstances make that impossible.'

'Oh,' said Crayshaw slowly. 'I see.' He looked at Hammond from beneath heavy lids, and went on quietly: 'I mean no discourtesy when I tell you that after my experience with Hilary in the past two years, I have little doubt that in a mood which is, I believe, called "ecstatic" by devotees of hashish and marihuana and kindred drugs, she tried to kill herself, and cunningly concealed the effect. Your are doubtless thinking of the absence of shoes and stockings; that merely proves that she had been dancing.'

Hammond sat back in his chair.

'Along the street?' he asked, 'without a mark on her feet?'

'Is that the case?' Crayshaw looked puzzled. 'There is doubtless an explanation—'

'No,' said Hammond, standing up abruptly. 'No, there's no explanation, except that her shoes and stockings were taken off either in my flat or before she was carried to the flat, and she was left to hang. Her handbag was examined, and something stolen from it, the loss of which terrified her because it was something of yours.'

Crayshaw looked at him with a queer, twisted smile.

'I have no doubt that the "something" will be found with the discarded shoes and stockings, Mr. Hammond. It is a small thing and a very simple one—a small, gold cross. It was her mother's, and she sets great store by it. Dr. Grunfelt, a psychiatrist who has been attending her for some time, went to considerable trouble to discover that to Hilary that cross is the symbol of purity. I—' he paused, 'I feel incapable of explaining as I would like to explain, yet I must try. In diseases of the mind—'

Hammond said: 'If you would keep the explanation to the case in point, rather than in general, it would be simpler.'

Crayshaw stared at him; Mike Errol stirred, as if in disagreement with Hammond's attitude.

'Of course,' Crayshaw said at last. 'In addition to the usual treatment, or "cure" for drugs, this symbol was likely to prove of great help. At Grunfelt's suggestion, I told her that if she failed in her good behaviour while carrying the cross, she would fail herself, and me, and that the punishment of mind she would suffer would be almost too great to bear. Unhappily in a mood of ecstasy she flings the cross away; twice it has been returned to me after the offer of a reward. But, of course, when she recovers from the mood and realises what she has done, she is frightened —your use of the word "terrified" was quite appropriate, Mr. Hammond. Does that make my certainty more understandable?'

Hammond hesitated, and then said: 'Well, yes, it does.'

'Did you advise the police?' asked Crayshaw smoothly.

'I didn't think that was necessary.' Hammond's voice was casual, but he was watching the other. The man's well-knit body appeared to relax, and he sipped again at the brandy. He did not try to hide a certain relief, but less, Hammond judged, than he felt.

'I'm glad, Mr. Hammond. It is distressing even to get the slightest publicity. I should not like to feel that Hilary was put under the jurisdiction of the law. I shall, of course, take even stronger measures to prevent a repetition of what must have proved a most trying incident for you, most trying.' He paused. 'Where did you find her?'

'In my flat,' said Hammond.

'Oh, I am sorry! I can easily understand your manner, your reluctances to believe the real explanation. You are an acquaintance of Hilary's?'

'No,' said Hammond.

'Then how did she get in?'

'How would she have got in had I been an acquaintance?' demanded Hammond.

'My dear young sir, presumably with a key.'

'Yes,' said Hammond, 'and that's how she did get in. But there are only two keys in existence, to my knowledge, and neither was used tonight.'

'What a puzzling business!' exclaimed Crayshaw. 'It's quite incomprehensible to me. Where do you live, Mr. Hammond?'

'At 50c, Jermyn Street.'

'At—' Crayshaw broke off. 'God bless my soul, how strange! Ferdinand lives there, on the third floor. He is Hilary's mentor, the man I mentioned. He—but perhaps you know him?'

'No,' said Hammond, 'but I propose to, quite soon. Will you come with me to Jermyn Street, sir?'

'Really, is that—'

'Necessary? I think so.' Hammond said brusquely. 'If you don't see him, the police will. I think he probably tried to murder your daughter, Mr. Crayshaw, whatever your personal opinion may be, but if you'll come I'll give him a chance to explain first.'

'Oh,' said Crayshaw. He paused, and Mike Errol thought he was about to make some kind of caustic rejoinder. Whatever it was, however, Crayshaw repressed. 'I am at your service,' he said gravely.

'Thanks,' said Hammond.

In silence they reached the Talbot. Even in it, except for refusing a cigarette, Crayshaw uttered no word.

Once in Jermyn Street, they left the car quickly and moved up to Hammond's flat.

'Stay put, Mark, will you?' Hammond called, and heard a distinct 'damn you, why?' as he went on up the stairs. He smiled to himself in the darkness, then reached a narrow landing. He had only been to the third floor of the house once or twice, and did not know it well.

Mike shone a torch.

'That's better,' said Hammond, and put a finger on the bell-push. They waited quietly; but there was no response. He tried again.

68

'I always understood that he kept a key on the lintel,' said Crayshaw at last. 'In view of the fact that I employ him, I feel we would be justified in trying to get in.'

'Good idea.' Hammond stretched a hand to the top of the door, and his fingers closed on a key. He held it out to Crayshaw: 'Will you use it?'

'No, no,' said Crayshaw hastily. 'Mine may have been the suggestion, but yours surely is the responsibility.'

Hammond inserted the key, turned it, and then felt the door give. It was quite dark inside, the dim beam from Mike's torch slipping furtively over the dull surfaces of shabby furniture.

Hammond groped for and found a light switch, then pressed it down. They were in a thread-bare hall, four doors leading from it and all of them ajar.

'Is anyone here?' Hammond called.

There was no answer.

'I hope that we are justified in entering in this fashion,' said Crayshaw, 'I have a wholesome respect for the police, and this intrusion might rank as unlawful entry.'

Hammond looked into the first room. It was empty. He tried the second, stepping in before the others, and half closing the door.

They heard his exclamation.

Fast upon it Crayshaw cried: 'What is it? What have you found?'

Hammond, ignoring the question, went slowly towards the bed. On it was a man whose right arm dangled to the floor. He had been strangled; his congested face, blue and purple, was dreadfully swollen. There was a cord about his neck similar to that which had been about Hilary's.

Hammond called softly: 'Come in, you two.'

Mike Errol urged Crayshaw forward. He entered the

room, hesitated, and then stopped abruptly, his eyes widening, his hands clutching his stomach. With a retching sound he turned blindly away.

'Let him go,' Hammond said.

Mike nodded. Crayshaw blundered across the hall and down the stairs. They heard him stumbling. His footsteps faded into the silence of the night, while Hammond and Errol approached the man on the bed.

It was Errol who said: 'That's odd.'

'What is?'

'That boot,' said Mike.

'Boot?' Hammond's voice rose as he followed the direction of Mike's gaze, and saw a boot, a heavy, hob-nailed one, lying on a small table. The boot had been ripped open; even the sole gaped from the uppers.

Hammond's thoughts were of Craigie's story, and Loftus's report, as he stepped slowly forward.

8

## QUIET NIGHT

There was not a great deal that either man could do.

Ferdinand was dead; and Hammond judged he had been dead for several hours. It was impossible to judge anything of the man's appearance, except that his hair was dark and that he was tall and thin. The grotesque distortions of his face were enough to turn any man's stomach; Crayshaw's reaction was hardly surprising.

Mike Errol helped Hammond to straighten the body, while looking at the other curiously. Hammond's manner, both at Crayshaw's house and the flat, was puzzling. Errol had an impression that much was going on behind those tired hazel eyes. There seemed little purpose in what Hammond had done, particularly in his manner with Crayshaw; but Mike did not doubt that the reason was sound. He felt a confidence in Hammond akin to that which he felt in Loftus, although this man was more difficult to understand.

With the ruined boot in his hand, Hammond turned to the door.

'There were a lot of things I forgot to ask Craigie,' he said.

'When I've come across deadoes during the past few years I've scarpered and concentrated on working up an alibi. I suppose I don't need to do that here?'

'Generally we get hold of Miller, at the Yard,' said Mike. 'He's liaison officer, or what serves for it.'

'Does he take orders?'

Mike grinned.

'Let's put it that he acts on suggestions.'

'A nice distinction,' smiled Hammond. 'I'm beginning to feel at home already. I wonder—' he paused in the doorway, then added irritably: 'I wish I weren't so damned tired. This needs such a hell of a lot of sorting out. Do you believe in coincidence?'

'Up to a point,' said Mike cautiously.

'Ye—es, well, I guess this passes it. I come home and find Hilary, confound her selfish heart, hanging behind my door. That's peculiar, to say the least of it. Crayshaw not only had a beautiful story prepared for us, but had spent some time working it up. Another coincidence—'

'There's no evidence that he was lying,' interpolated Mike.

'Who said there was? I'm just registering it as a coincidence that he had such a beautiful explanation ready for us. Grunfelt was that doctor's name, wasn't it?' He paused, and then went on: 'Coincidence three. Hilary's guide and counsellor lives in a flat immediately above mine, and coincidence four, hey-presto, here's the boot which Loftus thinks is up a tree!'

Mike stared at him.

'I'll make the outlines broader a little later on, Mike. Mean-while we've got to handle this thing as it comes.' He stopped abruptly, and added: 'Boots should come in pairs. Let's find the other.'

The search proved futile, for there was no sign of the other boot.

In his own flat, a brief résumé of what had happened was passed on to Mark, and then Hammond said: 'Will one of you 'phone this man Miller, at the Yard? And the other keep an eye open in case we get visitors? I'd like to try to get hold of Craigie.' This time, Craigie's quiet voice answered him.

Hammond talked at some length. When he had finished there was a short pause, before Craigie asked: 'What do you make of it, Bruce?'

'Not much. I think we ought to know all we can about Crayshaw, his daughter, Ferdinand and the good Dr. Grunfelt with the Teutonic name. As for making a pattern of them, I can't. I might be able to when I've had some sleep.'

'Then see you have it,' said Craigie. 'We can all get together in the morning. Leave the Errols to look after the details about Ferdinand—is that his Christian name?'

'I don't know,' said Hammond. 'That's another of the things I forgot to ask.'

'Let it rest for the moment,' said Craigie. 'Meanwhile sleep.'

Hammond stifled a yawn. 'Shall I tell the Errols to report to you?'

'If they've anything they think needs it,' said Craigie.

Hammond rang off a few seconds afterwards. He was too tired to think, almost too tired to undress. The dangling feet of Hilary Crayshaw, Ferdinand's face, flitted across his mind as he peeled off his clothes. He heard a murmur of conversation coming from the other room, then the voices faded and he slept.

In the other room, Mike was saying with unusual gravity: 'Bruce looks fit to drop, don't you think?'

'Fit to? He's dropped.'

'He must have had a hell of a time.'

'Craigie might know.'

73

'Ye—es,' said Mike, 'but I don't think we'll worry him with questions at the moment. What did Miller say?'

'He's not there,' Mark told him, 'but they're sending a sergeant over, and going through all the usual motions. I've asked 'em to put Ferdie in the morgue at Cannon Row, where we can have a look at him when we want to. I've taken everything out of his pockets, but there's nothing that signifies.'

'Too bad. We'd better take turn and turn about here for the night.'

'Yes,' said Mark crisply. He spoke more quickly than his cousin; that, together with the fact that he was not quite so even-tempered as Mike, and took things more hardly, was the main difference between them.

The police came; they asked no questions, and they took the body away. Though photographs were taken, and fingerprints located, it was understood that the Yard might know nothing more of what happened in the search for this man's murderer. They were specially selected men who worked in co-operation with Department Z. They would collate all the information possible, make all necessary and relevant inquiries, then pass the results through to Craigie, taking no further action unless requested to by him.

Nothing transpired at the flat that night.

Craigie was quickly in touch with several other agents, starting his inquiries into the Crayshaws and Ferdinand; by the morning he hoped to have information which he could pass on to Loftus and Hammond. He and Hammond would go to the nursing-home, meeting Kerr and Loftus there early the following afternoon.

He thought at length of Hammond.

He knew that the man had been hunted across the Continent, but had no idea of what had happened during the hunt. He did know that Hammond had said, just after entering the office, that he had not slept for seventy-two hours except for a short nap on the flying-boat from Lisbon. That meant he had been hunted even in Portugal.

I wonder, thought Craigie a little uneasily, whether he should have had a week's rest before starting this?

He let down a bed which was fitted into the wall of the office, and lay there looking at the dying embers of the fire. It was a long time before he slept.

When Hammond awakened, his body was tensed and expectant.

His right hand moved slowly beneath the bedclothes. He frowned, finding nothing; then he drew a deep breath and smiled toward the ceiling.

He had been groping for an automatic.

He had not slept without one by his side for many months. Now he remembered where he was, yawned, rubbed his eyes, and sat up against the pillows.

A breeze was fluttering the curtains at the window, and light was entering the room freely. Somewhere over the roofs of nearby houses the sun was shining.

He stretched himself luxuriously, then frowned. One of the Errols had entered the room during the night or earlier that morning, for when he had gone to bed the curtains had been drawn. It was disturbing to think that he had slept so heavily that he had heard nothing. The door opened cautiously.

Mike's sleek head appeared.

'I'll have my tea now, Errol,' said Hammond promptly.

Mike grinned. 'Very good, sir. Indian or China?'

'Indian, and piping hot.'

'Yes, sir.' Mike disappeared, and Hammond's smile widened.

They were good fellows, and it was surprising how easily they took a quip, how readily they did what he suggested, without asking questions or raising objections. He had not really understood the Department Z men in England; for the most part they were a different breed from those operating abroad.

Within five minutes Mike came in with the tray. Mark was behind him. 'Do you know what the time is?'

'Only the haziest idea,' admitted Hammond.

'Too hazy to take in five past eleven?' asked Mark airily.

Hammond's eye widened.

'Is it, by George! Care to run a bath for me?'

Shaved, bathed, and dressed he felt fresh and invigorated as he made his way to the kitchen. He found Mark bending over a frying pan from which an extraordinary assortment of smells was rising.

'We waited for you,' Mike said virtuously. 'You might put on the tablecloth.'

In five minutes they were sitting at the breakfast table; in twenty they had finished, and the clock on the mantel-shelf pointed to ten minutes to twelve. It was while the Errols were telling Hammond that all had been quiet, and nothing had happened, that the telephone bell rang.

'I'll get it,' said Mike. He pushed his chair back and went into the other room, only to call: 'Craigie, for you, Bruce.'

'Hallo, Craigie,' said Hammond a moment later. 'Yes, like a top ... yes, of course ... yes, I'll be there.' He replaced the receiver, singing out: 'I'm to go to Bob Kerr's place with Craigie, leaving the office at one o'clock.'

'Oh, you are, are you?' said Mark. 'What about us?'

'It wouldn't be a bad idea if you stayed here,' suggested Hammond. 'The police have made a search upstairs, I suppose, but it would be as well if you made a more thorough job of it.'

Mark grimaced.

'Yessir,' he said. 'Anything to oblige, sir.'

'Don't be an ass,' said Hammond a little uncomfortably. 'I— look here, I'm new to a lot of things. If Loftus were here instead of me, what would he suggest?'

Mike said promptly: 'Probably the same as you, and in any case he would clump Mark's thick head. You don't have to worry about us, old man. We always do as we're told.'

'I don't know what Craigie's arranged,' said Hammond. 'Leave it to me for the time being, will you?'

They nodded; and he felt much easier in his mind when, at a quarter to one, he left the flat.

A Daimler was waiting outside the small, hardly noticeable doorway in the side-street off Whitehall which led to Craigie's office. Countless people passed it every week, and few of them could have said, off-hand, that there was a doorway there. A pile of sandbags gave it a casual air of obscurity.

As Hammond drew up, Craigie appeared from behind them. He looked keenly at Hammond, and smiled, relieved to see that his fears that Bruce would be suffering too much from the fatigue of his recent escape were unfounded. 'We'll be about an hour and a half on the way.'

'Plenty of time for exchanging notes,' said Hammond.

'I haven't many,' said Craigie. 'The reports aren't in yet.'

'Anything arrived from Loftus?'

'No, except to tell me that the comb-out of the trees down there has started. I haven't told him about our boot,' Craigie added, without vouchsafing why. 'Well, Bruce, what do you make of it now?'

Craigie was driving through the traffic in Victoria before Hammond had marshalled his thoughts well enough to give a definite reply. Then he started a little hesitantly.

'It's a bit early, even for an interim report, but there are one or two things that stick out. The coincidence angle, for instance. Why was the girl in my flat, and how was it that Ferdinand had the flat above me? Also, why was the boot there? No one knew that I would be working on the case. No one could have known when Ferdinand first took the flat.'

'I've got that far,' said Craigie.

'We've got to face the fact that Ferdinand was working for the men who wanted Emile's message,' went on Hammond slowly, 'or at least that he was connected with them. It could just be a coincidence, but to my mind that's a little too coincidental to accept.'

Craigie waited.

Hammond went on: 'As far as I can work it out, it goes something like this: When I was rooted out in France, word was sent to the Nazi mob over here. I was known as a Department Z agent, and it was considered likely that I would come back to London. On that chance, then, Ferdinand was installed in the flat above mine. There was still a lot of information, such as the names of apparently pro-Nazi Frenchmen who've helped me, they would like to know.'

Craigie shot him a smiling, sideways glance. 'As a matter of fact Ferdinand moved in three months ago. I've thought pretty well on the same lines as you have, Bruce, and come to much the same conclusion.'

'Good!' said Hammond heartily. He looked and felt relieved. 'It disposes of the coincidence angle anyhow, and we can work on the basis that they knew I was back and thought it likely I would soon be at work on this side. Why they put the girl in my flat doesn't matter all that much. It may have been as an Awful Warning, or it might have been meant as a beautiful red herring.'

Craigie said: 'How?'

'Isn't it obvious? There was the possibility that I would

soon be looking for the boot. In any case, anything I found I would certainly have reported to you. They put the girl in my place to make sure I couldn't miss the business. The next step was obvious, too—I would make inquiries, or you would. We would get to Crayshaw, and certainly to Ferdinand. Ferdie had the boot. The connection between Emile, his boot, Hilary and Crayshaw might be obscure, but the chances are that they hope we'll take it for granted that there is a connection, and we'll work on that. Thus, the red herring. We're to be busy on the Hilary Crayshaw-Ferdinand angle, while they go on their own sweet way. Doesn't that look the likely explanation to you?'

Craigie pursed his lips. 'I don't think we should say more than it's a possible one, but you're probably right.' He was silent for some seconds, then added slowly: 'You start off with a premise we haven't really proved yet: that "they" put Hilary Crayshaw there. You've assumed that it was attempted murder, and not suicide?'

'I haven't a shred of doubt about it,' Hammond admitted.

'So you don't believe Crayshaw?'

'I wouldn't go as far as that. But he's wrong this time.'

'He could be lying,' murmured Craigie.

'I haven't lost sight of that possibility,' admitted Hammond.

'So if it's in mind as a possibility, we're going to need a watch on Crayshaw, one of the key men in armaments. Thus the red herring, if it is one, works to some degree,' said Craigie, 'always assuming that Crayshaw is straight.'

They lapsed into silence. Then Craigie said abruptly: 'Why did you let Crayshaw see Ferdinand, Bruce?'

## 9

## GET TOGETHER

Hammond raised one eyebrow a little above the other, then said with apparent candour: 'I don't quite know.'

Craigie made no comment.

'I wasn't impressed by Crayshaw's manner,' went on Hammond. 'There was something forced about it, and I wanted to see his reaction when he saw Ferdinand. I admit it was a bit more realistic than I expected. However, it'll be interesting to know what he does today. Also, I think the girl should be watched.'

'That's being done.' Craigie slowed down, and put out his right-hand indicator. 'All right, Bruce, so far our minds have worked in the same direction. There's just one thing that we should have clear. I don't want to try to make you work on lines that are uncongenial to you personally. We all have individual methods. I see you're brooding about Crayshaw, and you've given free rein to ideas which can't yet be called suspicion; you probably couldn't say just why.'

'No—o,' said Hammond.

'All I want to be sure of is, that as soon as you can say

"why", to this or any other thing, you will let me know. There's always the chance that you may be knocked out, and if that should happen, I need to have everything as up to date as possible. In our business no man should be indispensable. Apart from that, you've a free hand.'

'Thanks,' said Hammond appreciatively, and they fell silent.

The drive from the main road to the nursing-home was not a long one. It took a little over fifteen minutes before Craigie turned off the narrow lane and Hammond saw the house. At first glance it was a sight which made the heart leap, a sudden picture of Tudor architecture so perfect, so lovely, that it pushed all other thoughts aside. The sun was shining on the tiled roof with its green patches and others of a fresher red, where tiles had been replaced. Mullioned windows were open, and the front door also stood ajar.

By the side of the house stood an ambulance.

'That will be the ambulance they've brought Emile in,' said Craigie.

'I wonder if Loftus is here?'

'I doubt it. He would have 'phoned me from Weymouth before starting back, and he hadn't 'phoned by one o'clock.' Craigie pulled up outside the house, and they climbed out.

It was as they approached the porch, while birds were singing about them and a light wind was ruffling the trees, that they heard a cry.

It was sudden and abrupt. It was not of terror or pain, but more of alarm.

Hammond pushed the door open and stepped into a panelled hall. He heard footsteps. Someone, a woman, was disappearing up the stairs.

Hammond followed her quickly.

Craigie watched him, hesitated, then turned and went outside.

There was nobody in the grounds as far as Craigie could see, but he waited on the porch with a hand at his pocket.

Hammond saw the woman disappearing into a room on the right of a narrow passage. He went after her swiftly, breaking into a scene which so startled him that for the moment he could only stand and stare. It was at such difference with the house and its charming serenity.

On a bed a youth was lying, his eyes staring as if hypnotised towards the ceiling. In the wall just above his head was an arrow; each feather faithfully etched by a shaft of sunlight.

The woman Hammond had followed was half-way to the open window by which a nurse was standing, her back towards the bed and the newcomers. In the framework of the window was a second arrow, still quivering.

Hammond lunged forward, thrusting the first woman aside, reached the nurse and pushed her roughly out of the line of fire. He caught a glimpse of the trees and the gardens, and of something moving among the branches of the cedar; it looked like a large brown monkey, but that was illusion; it was a man.

Hammond dropped his hand to his right pocket.

He heard the quick breathing of the two women, but they did not move again. The sun glinted on his automatic as he brought it out. Then he saw the man near the cedar turn; he was standing close to the trunk, holding a small bow. He fitted an arrow to it with incredible swiftness, but before the *whang!* of the string could be heard, the sharp crack of Hammond's shot echoed about the room.

The bow whanged; the arrow, deflected by the shot, passing harmlessly over the roof. Hammond straightened up and fired again, but the archer was now on the move, slipping from tree to tree with verve and confidence.

Hammond heard Craigie call up: 'Come down quickly, Bruce!'

Craigie was running along the drive, with an automatic in his hand. Bruce hesitated just long enough to judge the chances of getting down from the window; they were good. He swung himself through, stood for a moment on the sill, and then slithered down the roof of the porch. Soon he was running in Craigie's wake.

The archer was fifty yards away from Hammond when Craigie fired. The man pitched forward, but picked himself up with a movement so swift and agile that it looked as if he had bounced to his feet.

Then he disappeared into a thicket of trees.

Hammond was overtaking Craigie, and did not pause as he passed his Chief. The trees had thinned out considerably and he could see his quarry, although only in glimpses and never clearly enough to provide a target. Another yard or so and Hammond saw that the man had found a gap large enough for him to get through, but too small for Hammond's bigger frame. He had to guess whether the man would turn right or left. The road along which he and Craigie had driven was on the right; Hammond took that direction, but as soon as he passed the bushes and saw the field ahead of him, he know that his guess had been the wrong one.

The field was large, and on the far side of it he saw his quarry scrambling over a hedge. Pursuit was likely to be a waste of time, and Hammond swung round.

He saw no trace of Craigie, but nearing the house his voice floated out from the hall. In a few seconds Hammond saw Craigie putting down a telephone-receiver, and regarding him with a half-smile.

'No luck?' he said, and then went on: 'I thought he'd get

83

away. Anyhow, the police will cover the roads as quickly as possible, but I doubt whether he'll be caught.'

Hammond glanced up at the woman he had hurled aside so roughly, who was slowly coming down the stairs.

'Hallo, Lois,' Craigie said quietly. 'This is Bruce Hammond. Bruce, this is Mrs. Kerr.'

Hammond decided that Kerr was a lucky man. Lois showed no sign of being ruffled, or inclination towards panic. She pushed pack a tendril of hair behind her right ear and held out a shapely, competent, entirely steady hand.

'Just Lois,' she said, simply, and turned her glance back to Craigie. 'You didn't get him, I suppose?'

'No.'

'Oh, well, he's only loosened a few tiles, and those he left intact Bruce took down with him.' Her eyes were laughing, but became suddenly serious. 'At least he didn't do Emile any harm.'

'Is the boy all right?' Craigie asked quickly.

'I think the nurse will be able to handle him,' said Lois, and Hammond thought she sounded a little puzzled when she said 'nurse'. 'He was frightened, but he didn't cry out.' She led the way into a long, low-ceilinged room. An enormous fire-place, deep and satisfying, took up a large part of it. 'How are you, Gordon?'

'I missed lunch,' Craigie said.

'Oh, confound you!' exclaimed Lois. 'I knew something like that would happen today; it's Bessie's afternoon off. It'll have to be something cold. For both of you?' she asked, looking at Hammond.

'A snack will do me,' he said. 'I had a late breakfast.'

'It's a contagious habit,' declared Lois. 'Now let me see— Christine won't be back for an hour or two. Bob rang up to say that he hoped to be here about half-past three, and Bill will be with him. But they'll have lunch on the road.' She hesitated. 'Will you come into the kitchen while I get it ready?'

Craigie smiled.

'If you expect to get a story out of Bruce with that simple ruse, you're wrong. He's closer than Bob ever was.'

'But I'm good at cutting bread,' said Hammond promptly.

'We may not come to that,' said Lois distractedly as they moved towards the kitchen.

He liked Lois's free and easy manner, the naturalness with which Craigie sat on a corner of the table and declared that he had no objection to watching, but he could be counted out for washing up. He was seeing Craigie, and others of the Department, in an entirely different and more human light than that in which he was used to seeing them, and he liked it.

They were sitting down at the kitchen table, at Craigie's insistence, when footsteps echoed along the red-tiled passage. They were quick and sharp, those of a woman; but there was a queer something about them which puzzled Hammond. They made him look curiously towards the door. He half-expected to see Loftus's Christine; he did not know whether Christine was engaged to Loftus or not, but was aware that their names were often associated.

It was not Christine; it was the nurse.

She had taken off her white cap and her dark hair was ruffled. The curious directness, and intensity of her blue eyes fascinated Hammond. He echoed, unconsciously, Loftus's first thought on seeing her: 'By George, she's lovely!'

He pushed his chair back.

'Please don't get up,' said Nurse Caroll. 'He's all right, now,' she added in answer to Lois's unspoken query, 'but I've promised to go up to him again in a few minutes.' She unrolled what appeared to be a folded pillow case which she had brought with her, exposing two arrows.

'I thought I'd better bring them,' she said rather primly, 'and there's one in the grounds, isn't there?' Hammond was fascinated by her voice, with its faintly husky note, and by the directness of her manner as she added: 'It ought to be brought in; it might be dangerous.'

'Dangerous?' Craigie asked.

'Yes. I don't know what they've been dipped in, but there's something.' She pointed to a stain which ran some two inches along the barb of the arrow, the whole of which was no more than nine inches long. 'Of course, it could be water, but I don't think it's very likely.'

Hammond was on his feet. 'Nor do I,' he said. He wondered why neither he nor Craigie had worried about the arrows; it had been Lois's arrival, of course, which had turned their minds from them. 'I'll go and look.'

Craigie smiled disarmingly at Nurse Caroll. 'We didn't come up for them, nurse, in case it disturbed Emile.'

'I gather that,' said Nurse Caroll quietly.

Hammond, by the door, felt an inward annoyance. Craigie had not overlooked the arrows; he alone was guilty of that, and he was tempted to admit it. He saw no point at the moment, however, in indulging in a spate of self-accusation, and decided to go on into the back garden. He had judged the lay-out of the house quickly, and guessed that the arrow would be in the vegetable garden, unless, of course, it had lodged in the roof.

He went forward, his thoughts travelling to the stain on the barb; why had the nurse been so sure of the possibility of poison? That was a little surprising, although poisoned arrows might spring to an imaginative mind, once the clue of a stain was there.

He was searching amongst some rows of cabbages when a quiet voice spoke from behind him.

Hammond spun round.

He knew it was the nurse, although he felt a queer stab of surprise when he saw her. She was standing quite close to him, and he imagined she was smiling a little, probably because of the way he had jumped.

'Shall we look?' she asked.

'It's a good idea,' admitted Hammond. 'I'd judged that it would be about here, but I don't know the lay-out too well.'

'Nor do I,' said the nurse. 'I only arrived here this morning.' She led the way towards a patch of grass between two marrow beds, and Hammond watched her walking, she had a smooth, easy grace, taking long strides which her full nurse's skirt made possible.

Then she stopped abruptly.

She did not exclaim, although Hammond did when he saw what had made her stop. A Scotch terrier was lying on the ground at the end of the marrow bed. The dog was stiff and lifeless, lying on its side so that they could see the almost hairless skin of its stomach. Its teeth were bared, as if it were snarling in death at whatever had injured it so mortally.

Close by, almost touching one of the legs, was the arrow.

The four of them gathered in the kitchen.

Hammond did not feel like finishing his meal, his hunger had quite gone. Lois had said little, but her face had paled when they had told her what they had found; the Scottie had been hers. She had gone to see him, nodding in Hammond's exhortation not to touch him.

Hammond had the arrow held in a handkerchief.

The nurse put on a kettle.

'There's no doubt about that stuff,' Craigie said a little needlessly. 'We'll get it examined as quickly as we can. The dog must have sniffed, and probably licked, it.'

The nurse turned from the stove, hesitated, and then said

very quietly: 'Please forgive me if I sound officious, but I was asked to come to look after Emile. I wasn't warned that anything like this might happen. If it's likely to again, I think someone should be at hand, don't you?'

Craigie said at once: 'Someone will be, I promise you.'

The nurse said gently: 'I'm making a cup of tea, is that all right?'

'An excellent idea.' Craigie rose from his chair and drew Lois aside. 'Just a moment Lois.'

They strolled from the room, leaving Hammond alone with the nurse. He watched her movements, each one quick, graceful, capable. Hammond felt a queer tightness at his breast as he watched her, knowing that he was staring but unable to stop himself. Then abruptly he said: 'Has Emile talked to you much?'

'Quite a lot, since yesterday,' she told him.

'Has he explained what happened to him?'

'Indeed, yes, poor child.' Her voice was practical and matter-of-fact, as she searched for cups and saucers. 'You haven't heard much about him?'

'Not enough,' he said.

She told him, without over-emphasis, all that Emile had said. Hammond listened to a picture drawn so vividly that he could almost feel the lad's terror, while he remembered his own flight, his own narrow escapes, dread hours of hiding in barns and lofts, and ditches as the Germans passed by. He waited until the nurse had finished and then said quietly: 'I can feel for him.' He might have been talking to himself. 'It's the modern equivalent to hell, and don't I know it.'

Her interest in him quickened.

'How can you know?'

He smiled crookedly. 'I've just come from France.' He

paused, and then went on: 'Nurse, you've gathered that this might be dangerous, haven't you?'

'Yes,' said Nurse Caroll, 'though I was hoping Emile would be all right from now on. His enemies must know he can do no more harm.'

'Ye—es,' said Hammond. 'Unless—' he paused, and his eyes grew eager, for he thought of the boot and the fact that he had assumed the 'enemies' had found the letter. If they had, would they worry about the refugee? His thoughts were a little confused, and for the first time he was unaware of Nurse Caroll's intent gaze.

Before he spoke again he heard a car snorting along the drive. He heard the brakes squeal and a door slam. Then a vast voice bellowed: 'Bless my soul, it's the old man himself! Hallo, Gordon!' There was jubilance in the voice, and it was explained a moment later as the voice went on: 'We've got it, the boot, the letter, the message, the lot!'

## 10

# THE MESSAGE

L oftus was easing himself from the Bentley as he shouted the words. The front door was wide open, and Craigie was standing in the porch.

Kerr was already approaching Craigie, and shaking hands.

Loftus put his stick to the ground, hoisted himself up, and came forward slowly but eagerly. He saw a movement behind Craigie, the flutter of a nurse's uniform, and the figure of a man whom he did not immediately recognise.

Then Hammond reached Craigie's side.

Loftus stopped short, raised his stick from the ground and waved it in the air.

'Hallo, Bruce!' The bellow sent a flush of satisfaction through Hammond, pleasure that he was recognised so quickly, that he was accepted with such obvious goodwill. Then he wondered whether Loftus knew what Craigie had already decided, and a shadow darkened his pleasure.

Loftus put his stick down and advanced, smiling widely. 'The past and the present meet, do they?' he said, and shook hands. 'May it be less of a curse for you than for me, my son.'

Hammond felt the shadows fading.

'Thank you for those kind words,' he said laughing.

'And now,' suggested Kerr, 'supposing we get to business?'

'Lead on!' cried Loftus.

His good spirits were boisterous, yet they were not irritating, as good spirits sometimes were. Hammond was thinking that since he had seen Loftus the man must have lost three stone. Yet the smile remained unaltered. The loss of his leg did not appear to have affected him unduly.

Not until they were grouped in comfort round the long, low sitting-room did Craigie tell Loftus and Kerr what had happened. He spoke before Loftus had taken the letter from his pocket, and Hammond saw something of the liveliness disappear from the big man's face.

When Craigie finished, Loftus asked an unexpected question.

'Was Nurse Caroll in Emile's room when it happened?'

'Yes,' said Craigie.

'The second arrow struck the window just as she reached it,' said Lois. 'It couldn't have been three inches from her face.'

'Good,' said Loftus, and it was clear to them all that he was relieved. Hammond looked at him quizzically, but like the others he asked no questions. There was little talk while Loftus took an envelope from his pocket and spread the letter out on his knee. Before he read it—and by then the letter itself was something of an anticlimax—he said quietly:

'We searched all the trees this morning, and found one boot. It was the right one, and the letter was under a sock in the sole. It doesn't give us as much information as we'd like, but it does tell us something. For the rest, two men were killed in the fight last night. One of them was the old woman's son Teddy, who was wearing the boots, the other was a Dr. Brice. The evidence from Welton, the policeman who managed to throw the boots away, suggests that at least four and possibly six men were engaged in the attack.'

Craigie nodded; no one spoke.

Hammond found his interest centring on the letter, for which so much had been risked. It was even possible to assume that it was the indirect cause of the murder of Ferdinand.

'Well, to the letter,' said Loftus. 'Decoded, here it is:

'"Further to message of February 19. Preparations are in advanced stage. Date believed to be April 21st but may be varied. Proceed with this to London immediately."'

There was no signature, and there were no explanatory notes. Both Craigie and Hammond leaned forward to examine it. The paper was soiled, brown and green in patches. One corner was torn, and there was a darker brown stain on one sheet of the paper, for there were two, the second being blank.

Lois broke the silence.

'We don't know much more, do we?'

Loftus gave a half-hearted grin.

'No, my poppet, but for you, more than enough. Bob, can't you convince her that the Department's plots are no matter for a soberly run nursing-home?'

'Enough of that,' said Kerr bluntly. 'This came to us, we didn't come to it, and for once I'll tell Gordon where he gets off if he tries to keep us out of it now. Anyhow, with Emile here, whether with your approval or not we're the centre of attraction.'

Unperturbed, Loftus said: 'Now we know.' He leaned back and closed his eyes. 'I'll say it,' he added. 'We know that the preparations are on a large scale, and we can assume that they're comprehensive. Germany's usually are. They're effective on or about the 21st of April. The only thing we don't know is the subject of them. Has anyone any ideas?'

'No more than you have,' Kerr said.

'I suppose,' Lois put in thoughtfully, 'it can't have anything to do with invasion?'

'There speaks the logical woman,' said Hammond suddenly. 'Obviously it could have, but I doubt it very much. I don't think Jerry will be able to muster men and material enough to have a shot at us this Spring. I doubt if he would even if he wasn't tied-up in Russia.' Hammond stopped, and the others looked at him without speaking. 'We're only guessing,' he went on. 'Why waste the time on it? Did you get the message of the 19th of February, Craigie?'

'No,' said Craigie, 'it didn't get through.'

Kerr said: 'Could Emile know about it?'

'The fact that they had a shot at him today suggests that he might,' said Loftus looking at Hammond.

'We—ell,' said Hammond, running a hand over his head, 'I had a talk with the nurse—Caroll, did you say she was called? Emile chatted quite a bit this morning. He told her that he had no idea what the letter was about, and that Legarde, or Langham, gave him no clue. The second sheet of paper,' Hammond added, 'in case anyone has the bright idea that it's written over in invisible ink, was put in to protect the actual letter. Emile put it there himself.'

Craigie spoke quietly, looking out of the window and giving the impression that he was uttering his thoughts aloud.

'We're not much further on than we were last night. It looks as if the other side thought there was more in the letter than there is. We may get word from one of the other agents, of course, but I wouldn't say that was likely.' He looked at Hammond. 'What do you think, Bruce?'

Hammond shook his head slowly.

'Nothing, yet,' he said. 'I'd like a talk with Emile; is there

93

any reason why I shouldn't stay here for a few hours, if not for the night?'

'No,' said Lois and Kerr together.

'Thanks.' Hammond looked at Craigie, who nodded. 'I'll do that, then,' he added, 'and we'll just watch results for the next twelve hours. You'll be taking care of the London end?' he added.

Loftus looked interested.

'Is there one?'

'I think I'll get back to town,' said Craigie, 'leaving you three to talk the matter over. If you're not coming back tonight, Bruce, give me a ring. If there's any news at all I'll call you.' He stood up, and they went in a bunch with him to the door.

'Ought you to go alone?' Hammond asked.

Craigie smiled, and Kerr said:

'He doesn't travel alone these days, we've taught him better.' He smiled at Hammond's look of enquiry, adding: 'There was a car behind you, although you probably didn't see it. We can't afford to lose our Father Confessor, so there's a system by which he's followed wherever he goes.'

Hammond realised the truth of this precaution as Craigie drove away. Faintly, discreetly, the purr of the following car came to them.

With the going of Craigie, Hammond felt curiously deflated. While Craigie had been there the anti-climax of the letter had not been fully effective; it was now. In consequence Hammond was silent for something more than ten minutes, and the conversation amongst the others was no more than desultory.

Then Lois said thoughtfully:

'I suppose there's nothing else for it, I'll have to leave you alone.' She grimaced at Loftus and Hammond, patted Kerr's cheek, and went out of the room. There was a short silence before Kerr stood up and closed the windows. Both he and Loftus looked at Hammond, and Loftus said gently: 'We can't be overheard, old man.'

'Oh,' said Hammond. He brushed his hair back from his forehead, and realised that they were waiting for his story of what had happened in London.

It had never been his habit to talk freely of his ideas, particularly when they were half-formed. Craigie had realised that, but Hammond felt he could hardly expect Kerr and Loftus to feel the same. To give them merely a brief statement of fact, as he would like to do, would suggest that he did not propose to take them into his confidence, and that was the last impression he wanted to create.

'We—ell,' he said, and somewhat hesitantly started the story. Before long he found himself plunging not only into the details, but the possibilities which they engendered. When he had told them what he had told Craigie, he added: 'We've got to watch the Crayshaw angle, whether it's a red herring or not. It's the fact that we're working so much in the air that worries me. We've nothing to bite on. The 21st April might mean anything or nothing.'

Loftus said: 'The inference is that there's a connection with activities in occupied France.'

'Is there?' asked Hammond. 'If so, it's the barest of possibilities. Personally, I'd taken it for granted that it was something that was going to happen over here. Something underground, perhaps. There's another possibility, you know. The Huns may have known more or less what was in that letter, and taken it as read that we would know what it was all about. If that's the case, it seems a wasted effort. Anyhow—' he paused, and then stood up. 'I think we ought to start from the fact that there are a number of agents in this country prepared to do anything to stop the letter getting through, and on that basis we're reasonably justified in assuming it's concerned with activities over here.'

'I haven't followed you,' said Kerr.

Hammond frowned, and Loftus said quietly: 'It's our old friend the hunch. I've heard of 'em, I've even had 'em.' He spoke soberly, without suggesting even by inference that it was useless to rely on hunches of any kind. 'Bruce, what did you think of the nurse?'

Hammond looked relieved at the change of subject.

'She's well above the average, isn't she?'

Kerr said: 'Bill's been harbouring dark suspicions of the girl.'

'Has he?' asked Hammond sharply. He felt a furious urge to defend Nurse Caroll, and forced himself to speak with a calm impartiality. 'That's why you wanted to know whether she was in the room, is it? The arrow near her face pretty well gives the suspicions their *quietus*, doesn't it?'

'Yes, and no,' said Loftus. 'If the swine wanted to get rid of Emile, they wouldn't mind who else died. We've proof of that with the doctor fellow, Brice. It's clear from papers found at his house that he's been passing information on for some time. He even kept a diary!' Loftus fingered his aluminium leg thoughtfully. 'Brice had to find out who had the boot, and where it was. He was at the hospital last night, talking to the regular physician there, a man named Shapgold. It was through him Brice learnt Emile's story. Brice started off at once, and managed to get through the Home Guard pretty easily, probably because he's a doctor.'

Hammond said abruptly: 'What Home Guard?'

'They were all over the place,' said Loftus. 'Good lord, yes! Why on earth didn't I think of that before?' He was staring at

Hammond, while Kerr looked from one man to the other, frowning a little uncertainly.

Hammond said: 'If you were stopped, Brice was probably questioned too. So what about the other four, five or six men? How did they get through?'

Kerr said slowly: 'Well I'm damned!'

'About the only people who could have followed Brice last night were other Home Guards, or military,' said Hammond, 'or men who passed for such. I'd better get down to see these Home Guard people. Are you two coming?'


It was not altogether a fruitless journey, although the results acquired were not as satisfying as the trio would have liked. It appeared that Home Guards from several districts were taking part in the manoeuvres, or more properly preparations for manoeuvres, which were to take place in about a week's time. Consequently, provided men had the correct pass-word and were in uniform they could pass through the lines without difficulty. Moreover, motor-cyclist despatch riders and, in some cases, radio cars with a driver and assistant and two radio-officers, also passed through without serious hindrance.

Hammond asked questions of dozens of men, found at the Home Guard H.Q., at private houses, clubs and meeting places. He was tireless and insistent. Loftus also did some questioning, and Kerr almost as much as Hammond. At half-past eight, when the night was quite dark, they met and compared notes.

Afterwards, Hammond said thoughtfully: 'It's quite clear now, anyhow. Our merchants had a radio-car, and got through on the strength of it. It passed just after Brice all along the road.'

'It was too dark to identify them,' Loftus said a little gloomily. 'We're not much further ahead.'

'Aren't we?' asked Hammond slowly.

Both men stared at him. 'Call it another hunch, if you like, but I think it might get us somewhere.'

'Don't hold it!' implored Loftus.

'All right,' said Hammond. 'I'm thinking it might be a good idea to find when the manoeuvres are really starting. These are dress-rehearsal preparations, and it's now the middle of April. Could the starting date be the 21st?'

## 11

## PROVISIONALLY THE 21ST

There was little chance of reaching the nursing-home again that night, for neither Kerr nor Hammond fancied a long drive through the black-out, particularly since a police priority call to Craigie elicited the assurance that there was nothing happening in London that demanded Hammond's return.

Over a late meal at a hotel, the trio talked desultorily over the whole range of activity during the past forty-eight hours. 'Of course,' Hammond said, 'it goes a lot further back than that. If only Langham could have had a word with me—' He broke off, scowling at Loftus. 'Have you ever felt that you'd like to be in a dozen places at once, as well as be in three or four different time cycles?'

Loftus leaned across the table.

'Not once,' he said, 'but a hundred times. The odd thing is, usually I've managed it.'

Hammond took a sip of an excellent white wine.

'You'll find that it's possible,' Loftus went on quite seriously. 'Craigie works the miracle. When you see him again, he'll be able to give you a précis of what's been happening, and what's been discovered. Any report which might apply to this show will be tabulated and reduced to the essentials. Langham's old reports, your own, any others from Europe over the past few months. Crayshaw will be written up, so will his daughter. Ferdinand will be checked thoroughly, with his friends and relations. What's more, Craigie will have a summary of the essential points in all of them, written in straightforward language that can't be misunderstood. Don't worry about your limitations, Bruce. The jobs will be done as well as if you'd done them yourself.'

He paused, and Kerr said: 'That's true.'

'You won't find it easy to understand at first,' said Loftus. 'You'll wish to hell you could have followed up each line personally, but after a time you'll realise that in effect you have. Tell the boys what you want, and they'll go to the limit to get it for you.' Another pause. 'Bob and I included.'

Hammond said slowly: 'I'm beginning to see what you mean.'

'Just at the moment,' said Loftus, 'you can't get it out of your mind that you, personally, seem to be doing very little, and that all the things are being done for you, or in spite of you. The Ferdinand murder and the Hilary outbreak don't seem to link up. They appear to be unrelated incidents, which—'

Hammond smiled. 'You're right enough in parts, old chap, and I don't suppose anyone's more right than that.' He finished his wine, and returned with renewed vigour to a Welsh-rarebit. The conversation became general and, because they planned to be on the road by seven o'clock next morning, they went to bed soon after half-past ten. Hammond entered his room first, and a few minutes afterwards heard voices in the next room.

Loftus was saying: 'Hammond's going to be good, Bob.'

'He is good,' said Kerr.

Hammond did not know that with the brief exchange Kerr and Loftus had completed his transformation from an agent of the Department to its operational leader.


Christine Weston, who had once played a great part in Loftus's recovery after the injury in which he had lost his leg, was sitting with Lois Kerr in the long living-room of the nursing-home. The red embers of a dying fire glowed on the faces of the two women, one near-beautiful, both charming, and both heart and soul in the work of the Department.

They were not, however, talking about the Department now.

'I asked her to come in here for a breather,' Lois was saying, 'She's been on duty for hours. What *is* there about her?'

Christine said: 'I wonder if she's married?'

'Or whether she's lost anyone? Bob told me her brother was killed in France, but surely that's too long ago to affect her so lastingly. She seems to be burning up inside.' Lois smiled at her own inability to find the right word. 'You know what I mean?'

'Yes,' said Christine. 'I—' she paused for a fraction of a second, and then added in a slightly louder voice: 'I wish they were coming back tonight.'

Lois said quickly: 'Ned Oundle's outside somewhere, with one or two of the other men.'

She looked over her shoulder, for the door had opened.

Nurse Caroll's voice came to them over the shadowy room. 'Can I take you at your word, Mrs. Kerr?'

'Another second and I'd have come up to find you,' Lois said. 'Pull that chair up, we're just going to have some coffee.'

Christine said more quickly than she intended: 'Chatting of this and that, we wondered why you had taken up nursing?'

A slow smile curved the nurse's lips.

'What else can I do? I can ride a horse, of course, and I'm told I have the figure and deportment for a model.' She shrugged. 'Oh, and I can play the piano fairly well, and do all the things convention expected before the war, but now—'

She broke off abruptly, for Bessie came in with coffee. Lois and Christine said nothing until the maid had gone and then Christine said bluntly:

'How long have you felt, well, as bitter as that?'

'Since my brother was killed,' said the girl quietly. 'I started nursing at once. Then in the early bombing my parents were killed.' She paused. 'I've just gone on, since then. I've found it easy to help others, possible to make friends among the patients. The only trouble is that they come and they go.' There was another silence, except for the homely sound of Lois pouring coffee. The girl went on very quietly: 'Emile's very like my brother. Have you ever felt there's something you must do, you can't rest until you've finished it? I want to get that boy well. I'm going to get him well,' she added, and then took a cup from Lois. 'Thank you, Mrs. Kerr.' She was smiling a little. 'That's all there is, I'm afraid. Nothing at all exciting.'

Lois said: 'We all feel the same way—all of us here, anyhow. You won't need telling that the men are on special work. That means complete and almost inhuman concentration until a job is finished. When it's done they find another.'

'Ye—es,' said Nurse Caroll: 'I was wondering earlier whether there was any way I could help them?'

Christine said quickly: 'There may be. We'll ask them when they get back.'

She led the conversation into different channels, while with Lois she wondered whether they had been right to pierce the enigmatic façade, and glimpse the bitterness and sense of grievous loss within.

While Hammond and the others were eating, Lois, Christine and Nurse Caroll drinking coffee, Ned Oundle and two other agents of the Department patrolling the grounds of the nursing-home, many other things were happening up and down the country.

There was, for instance, a nation-wide search for the little man who could climb a giant cedar, and draw a bow and arrow with such unpleasant accuracy. The records and the social acquaintances of the dead Dr. Brice were being meticulously investigated. Two young agents were following up the Crayshaw angle, daughter and *père*. Superintendent Miller, of Scotland Yard, and yet another agent of the Department were going closely into Ferdinand's life and, as it happened, making more progress than any of the others.

At the same time Gordon Craigie was at Number 10, Downing Street, in close conversation with the Rt. Hon. Graham Hershall, Prime Minister.

Hershall was standing in front of the fire, his hands behind his back, thrusting his powerful chest and thickset shoulders forward. His round face, with its rosebud mouth and rather deep-set eyes, was frowning. From one corner of his lips jutted a cheroot, unlighted.

'All right, all right,' he said. 'I'll grant you that you're convinced it's serious, Craigie, but surely you can give me something more definite than that?'

'Not yet,' said Craigie. 'I'm hoping you can give me something.'

Hershall scowled. 'Now you're trying to tell me there's something you don't know.' His eyes were twinkling, for he was in a good humour, the scowl wholly assumed. 'Just what are you after?'

'I want to know of anything that might be planned here on the 21st of the month,' said Craigie.

Hershall looked up sharply, hesitated, and then said slowly: 'The twenty-first of April—' he peered towards the ceiling. 'Let me see now, there's a big-scale invasion exercise, provisionally fixed for the 21st.'

'Where?' asked Craigie bluntly.

'Is the South of England enough for you?'

'It seems it will have to be,' Craigie said. 'There's nothing else at all?'

'Nothing I can think of that's big enough to make you worry as you are doing,' said Hershall. 'The exercise is going to be a big one—to quote the Press, the biggest yet held in this country! Except that this time the Press won't be quoting it, until it's over.'

Craigie let that hint pass.

'There *is* another thing, Craigie. So secret that only three of us know the date, yet—Brookham, Westerham and myself.' Brookham was the Minister of Supply, Westerham one of the members of the Supply Mission to Moscow in the previous autumn. 'We're having a conference on the 21st for the full and final reports on all supplies.'

'How many will be at the conference?' asked Craigie.

'About a dozen.'

'Can you name them?'

'Yes, I can. Oh, damn you, Craigie, you'd get blood out of a stone, or information out of the Foreign Under-Secretary!' Hershall's grin was almost boyish. 'The three I've named, Lessington, Cator, Brille, Cavendish, Muire, Kenley, Crayshaw and Uppingham. There'll probably be two or three others. Mind you, none of them know that it's coming off yet.'

'Can you be quite sure of that?' asked Craigie. He was thinking of Crayshaw, and he spoke so quietly that Hershall said:

'What's that?'

Craigie repeated it, and Hershall pursed his lips.

'It depends what you mean by quite. Most of them know that such a conference is inevitable sooner or later, and they probably think it will be sooner. Why?'

'There could be a plan to break up the conference,' said Craigie. 'How long have you had it in mind?'

'For some time,' admitted Hershall. 'Y'know, Craigie, you're a damned disturbing fellow. There shouldn't be a leakage of information about this, but I can't guarantee there hasn't been.'

'It isn't going to surprise me if we find one,' admitted Craigie. He tapped out the bowl of his meerschaum and stood up. 'So there's the conference and the manoeuvres, both starting on or about the 21st. The probability is that this business is connected with one or the other. How long has the date of the manoeuvres been known?'

'Oh—say a month.'

'And the conference?'

'About the same. I'm not going to tell you, Craigie, that I don't want your fellows to know definitely about this, with the few exceptions you may think necessary. Keep them both covered up all you can, won't you. No need to say that,' he added with a smile. 'Is there anything else?'

'No, thanks,' said Craigie briefly, and then paused: 'Well, yes, there is. Where's the conference being held?'

'It's not yet decided. Either at Cavendish Hall or Crayshaw's place in Dorset. Probably Crayshaw's,' added the Prime Minister. 'We'll be at hand to inspect some of the troops at the manoeuvres then. You needn't ask the next one—

JOHN CREASEY

Crayshaw hasn't been approached, but we've used his place several times without much notice. Excellent location tucked away in the wilds of Dorset, and it's fairly near to London.'

'Ye—es,' said Craigie, soberly.

He was suddenly perturbed because of these conferences of great importance which had taken place at Crayshaw Grange before, conferences of which vital information had leaked out, and given much trouble. He had known that Hershall and Crayshaw were personal friends, but had not known how much the Prime Minister relied on the industrialist.

He left Number 10 soon afterwards, and walked into Whitehall. It was a clear night, and the moon was just setting, lending an eeriness to the majestic buildings. He heard the movements of sentries and policemen, saw an occasional taxi pass him, waited for a moment on the kerb and then walked across the road towards his own office.

As Kerr had said, Craigie was always accompanied on long journeys; but he did not think that necessary on short ones. Certainly he was not thinking of danger as he reached the opposite pavement.

A constable approached him, and the light of the man's torch shone full into Craigie's face.

'Good night, sir.'

'Good night,' said Craigie, still blinking from the glare.

He had to use a torch to show him the entry between the sandbags leading to his office, and consequently he saw the man who was standing there a split-second before he would otherwise have done.

It did not occur to him that it could be any other than one of his own men, waiting because he had been unable to get into the office.

'Hallo,' he said, and raised his torch.

It was then that the man hit him.

The blow was delivered to the jaw, a short-arm jab of considerable force. Craigie thudded back against the sandbags. His hand flew automatically to the gun in his pocket. At the same time he felt the sting of acid biting into his eyes, his nostrils, as it seared through his breathing, penetrating to his very lungs. He tried to strike out but could not, nor could he make a sound except an incoherent whispering deep in his throat.

A second blow fell savagely on the back of his neck, and he lost consciousness.

Two men emerged from the shadows of the sandbags, half lifting, half dragging Craigie's body to a waiting car.

The men bundled Craigie in, climbed after him, and slammed the door. The car moved off slowly, passing a constable who turned into the street. The constable passed the sandbags and, a few seconds afterwards, felt his eyes smarting. Tear-gas, he thought, or one of the nose and throat irritants.

It was odd, for there had been no gas test in the neighbourhood that day.

For safety's sake he put on his mask, then went to the sandbags. He raised the face-piece of his mask cautiously. Here, undoubtedly, the smell was stronger. He went into the building, but no one was there, and there was no hint of the gas actually inside the hall or staircase. Never-the-less he was alarmed enough to telephone a report to the Yard immediately. When the investigators arrived, however, the smell of gas had gone.

Someone suggested that a trial tube of gas had been released by accident, and the matter was referred back for attention the next day.

Craigie, meanwhile, was taken out of London.

He came round while he was in the car, but found that his

limbs refused to move when he tried to direct them. When eventually the car stopped outside a house which he could only just see in the darkness, he could not walk by his own volition, and was half-carried into the building.

The stairs were quite beyond him, and the man who had first attacked him carried him up. Craigie saw vaguely that the staircase was a wide one; he knew no more than that. He was taken into a brightly-lighted room, and dropped into an easy chair.

'Excellent work, Blaker, excellent work indeed.'

Craigie only just distinguished the words and the muttered answer. He saw the man who had carried him go away, and heard the door close. He closed his eyes, then opened them gradually, in an attempt to get a clearer vision. A bearded face appeared before him, one moment seeming close to his face, another receding so far that he could see the whole of the man's head. Presently the beard, the pale cheeks and high forehead, grew recognisable.

Craigie gripped the arms of his chair.

'I think you will be much better here for a while, Craigie, don't you? Besides, I think you can help me.'

Craigie was thinking: My God, it's Crayshaw.

The idea, at first fantastic and turbulent, gradually settled to a grim acceptance. He did not doubt after the first few minutes that it was Sir Noel Crayshaw; beyond that he could not think.

## 12

# SENSATION IN HIGH CIRCLES

Mike and Mark Errol, weary of work which showed little result, tired and irritable in consequence, regarded one another from easy chairs on either side of the fireplace at their flat.

Mark said gloomily: 'This is a ruddy fine show. No sign of—'

'Craigie, Hammond, Loftus—'

'Or any of them,' completed Mark. 'Where the hell has Craigie got to, that's what—'

'The trouble is, in this show,' said Mike, 'that everything's out of line. It would be better if Loftus was on the prowl.'

'No, Hammond's all right—'

'Who said he wasn't?' growled Mike. 'It's just that he's new, and that naturally upsets things. I can't remember a time before when Craigie hasn't answered in ten hours.'

'I'd better ring him again,' said Mark, hopefully stretching out his hand for the receiver. As he did so the telephone bell rang sharply.

Considerably startled he lifted the receiver to his ear. 'Hallo... hallo...'

'Errol? ... This is Hammond, d—n—o—'

'Call it said, old chap. What's up?'

'Have you heard from Craigie recently?' Hammond demanded.

'No,' said Mark, and all facetiousness left him. 'We rang him at midnight, and it's now 10 o'clock. We've tried pretty well once an hour.'

There was a sharp and urgent note in Hammond's voice: 'Get in touch with as many of the others as you can. Ask them whether they've had word from him since midnight. Get Miller of the Yard to find where he was last seen. Got that?'

'Yes,' said Mark crisply. He replaced the receiver, turning a thoughtful face to his cousin. 'Trouble. They can't contact with Craigie either ...' He dialled another number. 'Hallo, Wally? Mark here ... have you tried to 'phone Craigie recently? ... twice this morning, yes ... I don't know yet, but Hammond seemed anxious ... cheer-ho.' He replaced the receiver again, and said: 'Try the other 'phone, Mike. I'll have a word with Miller.' He dialled the Yard while Mike started a round of calls on the other telephone. One after another agent said the same thing: they had called Craigie to report, but had received no answer.

The Errols regarded each other blankly. At last Mark said: 'Well, we needn't stop working. You're following Hilary this morning, remember?'

Leaving Mark with the telephone literally at his finger tips, Mike went off to Audeley Street. A man reading a newspaper in the driving seat of a Lancing nodded. A few minutes afterwards he drove off, and the place by the kerb was taken by a taxi. This was driven by a second agent of Craigie's, a man

Mike would be able to use if there was need for leaving Audeley Street by road.

Mike was half an hour doing nothing.

Then the door of number 177c opened, and he saw the girl. She turned towards Piccadilly. Mike followed her as she walked rapidly towards Kensington Gardens.

There were enough people about to enable Mike to do this without much risk of being seen. He had wondered once or twice whether it would not be wiser for someone Hilary did not know to follow her, and with this in mind, kept the distance between them a good fifty or sixty yards.

He had little doubt that she was going to an appointment; there had been nothing hesitant about her manner; she knew just where she was going, and why.

Mike waited near a bridge over the Serpentine as the girl walked to the far side.

'Place of appointment, otherwise the rendezvous,' murmured Mike. Trees and shrubs gave him ample cover, and he was able to watch her without the slightest risk of being seen.

He saw her stiffen.

Half a dozen people were walking towards her. One of them, a man of medium height, wearing a light blue suit, stopped. Mike saw his rather heavy face, and mop of untidy reddish hair. Man and girl talked quickly for several minutes, Hilary gesticulating from time to time as if in protest.

Mike approached slowly, taking what cover he could behind trees and shrubs.

Hilary's voice floated out to him, furious, outraged. 'But I must have it, I tell you! I've paid for it, haven't I?'

'They didn't give it to me,' the red-haired man said sullenly. 'It's no use talking like that.' He looked away from her evasively, and Mike glimpsed his expression. In it he caught something more than sullenness; it was as if the fellow was waiting for something, was on edge for a development which might come at any moment.

Footsteps passed Mike, but except for the girl's voice raised in pleading there was no other sound; until Mike suddenly became aware of movement some ten feet in front of him.

He saw a man in a greenish brown suit, in colour barely distinguishable from the trees. He was taking what appeared to be a fishing-rod from a canvas case.

Mike started; and something of what Craigie had last told him flashed through his mind. He saw that the 'fishing-rod' was actually a bow, that the man was fitting a little gaily-feathered arrow into position.

There were ten feet and a small tree between Mike and the archer. The tree would prevent him reaching the man, and in any case what he knew of the dead dog warned him that he must not take the risk of being scratched by the arrow.

Slowly, being careful that a sudden movement wouldn't catch the eye of the archer, he raised his gun.

As he did so the man fixed the arrow and drew back the string. The gesture, once the bow was fitted, was startlingly fast, so fast that Mike felt a sudden tearing anxiety lest his caution had made him too late.

He fired at the man's legs.

The bark of the shot, the twang! of the bow, the whirring of the arrow as it sped towards the man and the girl, all merged together. The man in green turned round, with a sudden fury; Mike knew the bullet had struck his leg, but for that split second the pain appeared to have no effect. He saw the man snatch another arrow from a sheath, and fling it towards him.

Mike ducked, and fired again.

Something brushed his hair, scraping along his scalp. He was afraid as he had never been in his life, but he saw that his second bullet had taken the archer in the chest. The man toppled slowly forward; as he went down, the point of one of his arrows scored a line of skin from his hand.

Mike left him, breaking from his cover towards Hilary Crayshaw, who stood staring down at her companion's face, distorted in agony. His arms and legs were lashing out, while from his cheek stuck the little arrow with its gay feathers.

The girl seemed hypnotised.

Slowly but deliberately she put a hand towards the arrow, but before she touched it Mike reached her, and flung her to one side. She fell against the railing of the bridge, all the breath knocked out of her.

From somewhere not far off a police whistle was blowing, while a woman stood at the far end of the bridge, screaming. The monotony of her cries, rending the air, acted like a jagged saw on Mike's nerves. A group of auxiliary fire service men were running from the banks of the Serpentine towards the bridge, while several policemen were making a good speed towards the fallen men.

Mike gripped the girl's arm.

She stared at him, recognising him. She had been afraid before, but not so desperately as she was now. Mike said harshly: 'Leave all the talking to me.'

She did not answer by word or sign, and before he could speak again the police had arrived.

Mike put a hand gingerly to his head.

The poison had worked with such speed on others that he did not think there was any serious chance that he had been affected, but he started when he touched something in his hair. He drew out one of the feathers, stared at it, and then raised his voice: 'Don't touch a thing.' His command was so urgent that the policemen who had arrived stopped dead. 'Not a thing,' he repeated, and went towards the shrubs.

He could just see the man, moving less violently now; he of the sullen face was not moving at all.

A sergeant approached Mike, who said more quietly: 'There are arrows about, Sergeant, tipped with poison. Don't let your men touch them. If I were you I'd even be careful about touching the bodies.' He took out his wallet and extracted a card, signed by the Chief Constable of Scotland Yard. 'I'd like a full report sent to Superintendent Miller as quickly as possible.'

'Yes, sir.'

'And I think I'd better have one of your men to come with me and the lady,' said Mike. His suggestion was shrewd, for he did not imagine the sergeant would be too easy about allowing him to remove Hilary. 'He can stay with us until you've had the all clear from the Superintendent.'

'Thank you, sir. You'll want a cab?'

'Yes,' said Mike, 'but it must be a man you know.'

The police found a taxi driver, and through a quickly gathering crowd Mike hustled the girl away. He knew that the dead men would be taken to Cannon Row; that he—or Craigie or Hammond—would have access to anything found in their pockets. His main task was to get Hilary Crayshaw to talk.

He had little doubt of what had been intended.

The furtive anxiety in the sullen eyes of the red-haired man had been evidence enough that he had known of the presence of the archer, and that the arrow had been intended for the girl. The explanation appeared to be simple enough, although horrible beyond imagining.

An appointment with the girl, so that she could be shot while talking; yes, that made sense.

Other things did not. For instance, why had that particular place been chosen? Mike asked himself that question as the girl sat back in the cab with closed eyes. She had lost all colour, and was breathing heavily.

Mike thought, I suppose it was as good a place as any; excellent cover, too, for the fellow to get away.

He noticed that the girl's eyes were now open, and that she was regarding him without expression; the terror she had evinced earlier appeared to have lost itself in something akin to stupor. He offered her a cigarette, and, rather surprisingly, she took it.

'One way or another,' Mike murmured, hoping to raise some spark, 'you aren't having too good a time, are you?'

She stared at him sluggishly, and then spoke very slowly and deliberately.

'I'm having a *hell* of a time.'

'It often comes in patches,' said Mike. 'Anyhow, when we've been to the flat and you've had a pick-me-up, we can see what can be done about putting it to rights.'

She shrugged. 'I can't do anything else. But—why should they kill Eric? First Ferdy, and then Eric.' Mike saw that she thought the arrow had been intended for her companion. It might be wise to let her continue thinking that way. He wished he could 'phone Craigie. Without Craigie he was like a ship without a rudder.

Loftus and Hammond would have helped, but he had no idea how long they would be in the country.

The cab pulled up outside his Brook Street flat, and the policeman who had been sitting next to the driver jumped down.

'Unless there's anything you want, sir, I'll wait down here.'

'There's nothing at the moment,' said Mike. He searched his pockets for the key, but before he had found it the door opened and Mark appeared. Together they helped the girl up to the first floor landing. The door of his flat, marked '2', was standing ajar, and he urged the girl through.

Then Mike started.

'Great Scott!' he exclaimed. 'Bruce, are you welcome! But—damn it, you were in Weymouth an hour ago.'

'An hour and a half,' said Hammond quietly. 'I flew up. I'm worried about C.' He paused. 'What's been happening?'

Mike said briefly: 'Leave it for a couple of minutes, will you?' He stepped to a cabinet and poured Hilary a stiff whisky and soda; she took it eagerly. It brought a little colour to her cheeks, and a good deal more animation to her manner.

She turned to Hammond. 'I was meeting a friend and he was killed.' She paused, then went on, furious at Hammond's lack of astonishment. 'Don't you understand? He was *killed!*'

'I'm sorry,' Hammond said simply. 'I can't say much more, I'm afraid. Are you feeling better in yourself?'

'I'm feeling damnable,' she said, and then laughed on a high-pitched note; the effect could surely not be wholly due to the whisky. 'Everything's damnable, it's hellish! I don't even know where I am, what I'm doing, all my friends are getting killed, and he—he *hates* me.' A look of shrewish cunning crossed her face. 'He hates me; sometimes I think he's driving me mad, mad, mad!' She screeched the last word, and then swung round.

Standing motionless in the doorway Hammond saw Crayshaw. He was surprised enough himself to start; but he was not prepared for the effect on the girl. She began to laugh, horribly, erratically, the pitch going higher and higher as it shook her whole body.

'Now Eric's dead, dead dead!' The words were just distinguishable. 'You always hated him, always. I'm not coming back to the house. Never again, never again!'

Crayshaw's voice broke through, quiet, authoritative.

'All right, my dear, if you don't want to come back I'm not going to press you.' He shot a glance towards Hammond, as if asking for co-operation. 'But there's always a home for you, when you want it.'

'I don't want it!' she shouted. 'I don't want to see you again; I won't see you!'

Crayshaw's shoulders appeared to droop, an immense resignation touched his features.

'All right, Hilary,' he said. 'All right.'

He began to walk down the stairs, Hammond following. Once on the pavement he looked at Hammond, and Hammond saw, or thought he saw, behind the droop, the resignation, a gleam of calculation, as if Crayshaw was thinking: is this man deceived? Have I succeeded in deluding him?

Crayshaw said: 'This is most distressing, Mr. Hammond. I can't understand how she should be with your friends again, but since she appears to place some degree of confidence in you and them, can I ask for your help? Can I rely on you to make sure that she gets into no more trouble?'

Hammond said: 'I think so, Crayshaw.'

'I cannot say how much I appreciate that! I wish—'

'My friends were concerned for Hilary, Crayshaw. An attempt was made on her life.'

'On—her—*life?*'

'Another attempt,' said Hammond. 'It's quite impossible, even if it were advisable, to keep the matter from the police this time.'

Crayshaw pressed a hand across his forehead. 'I see. Very well, Mr. Hammond. I will arrange an interview with the

Home Secretary. I must not let her be placed under arrest, or charged.'

'With what?' Hammond flashed.

'Why—taking drugs, of course.' Crayshaw looked at him as if surprised. 'Surely there is nothing else?'

'No,' said Hammond. An oblique glance showed him a grey-clad figure whom he recognised as a Department Z agent. He nodded slightly, and then looked back at Crayshaw. 'I can't stop now,' he said, 'but I'll 'phone you as soon as I can.'

'Thank you,' said Crayshaw gravely. 'I know that I do not have to stress the anxiety which I feel.' He bowed gravely, then stepped towards a Daimler limousine drawn up some distance along the road.

The man in grey, meanwhile, had approached the taxi driver. Hammond was satisfied that Crayshaw would be followed, and went back to the flat. Mike and Mark were looking helplessly at Hilary.

She was stretched out on the settee, her eyes closed, her breathing stertorous. Now and again her whole body twitched.

Mike said: 'She wants a doctor, and a nurse.'

'Ye—es,' said Hammond, and looking towards Hilary he saw a different face on her shoulders, a pair of very blue eyes, and dark, ruffled hair. 'Yes,' he said more crisply, 'she wants a nurse. I think I know a good one.'

Mr. Augustus Cator looked across the large office in Throgmorton Street and said irritably: 'I wish Crayshaw would come; he's put this off too long already.'

The two men with him, Lord Muire and Sir Andrew Uppingham, nodded without speaking. They shared Cator's annoyance with Crayshaw, but disliked Cator enough to avoid saying so. A small, thin-faced man, Cator was inspired by a zeal which the others could not understand. He was always impatient, always urging greater efforts, always dissatisfied.

Muire and Uppingham, like Cator, controlled large munition combines, and with Crayshaw were on the list of those likely to be present at a conference on the twenty-first of April. Large men, red-faced, very much alike, they could not associate themselves with Cator's restless energy, although they were uncomfortably aware that production was not as good as it should be. They were fully aware of their importance; they knew that with Crayshaw they were directly responsible for a large proportion of munitions output. They were afraid that Crayshaw was going to lean towards Cator, demanding greater exertions and even forcing action. They believed good results could only be obtained gradually; they were averse to stunt methods and artificial stimulation to output.

They had another thing in common with Cator; they were personal friends of Crayshaw.

After ten minutes, Uppingham said: 'Of course, he's very worried about his daughter. She is giving more trouble than— yes?' He broke off at a tap at the door.

A man came in, dressed in commissionaire's uniform. They did not know him, for it was Crayshaw's office. He saluted respectfully, saw them gathered about the table, and approached.

'What is it?' asked Uppingham testily.

The man drew a hand from his pocket.

'I thought you would like to see this,' he said, and dropped what looked like a small glass ball to the table.

He moved with extraordinary speed to the door, slamming it behind him. The key turned in the lock. Almost immediately, the ball burst, emitting a sharp, acrid smell, which bit at the nostrils of the three men. Worse; there followed a smell of geraniums, that dread odour familiar to them all.

Coughing, they groped their way to the door, to find it locked. They staggered towards the windows, but the room was now filled with gas, and they did not succeed in opening them.

They were dead within two hours.

## 13

# SEARCH FOR CRAIGIE

L oftus, sitting at Craigie's desk, looked up at Hammond with narrowed, worried eyes. The tall man's stick was lying across the desk, and one of Craigie's writing pads had been opened; a series of hieroglyphics covered the top page, and Loftus's pencil still moved aimlessly about them.

'Yes,' he said. 'I don't see why you shouldn't use Nurse Caroll. We've found that Brice heard about the boots from Shapgold, and Shapgold from the matron, so that clears her. If she'll come, mind you. She might prefer to look after Emile.'

'I should think Lois Kerr could persuade her,' said Hammond. 'I'd like her to handle Hilary, if it can be arranged. I suppose I'd better 'phone from here.'

Hammond put through the call and since Department Z always had priority, was connected very quickly. Christine answered him; Hammond did not know her, yet, for he had flown from Weymouth with Loftus on news of Craigie's absence; only Kerr had gone to the nursing-home.

Christine said: 'She's out in the garden with Mrs. Kerr and Emile. Can I give her a message?'

'Hold on a moment, please,' said Hammond, and passed the instrument to Loftus.

'Bruce wants Nurse Caroll up here,' Loftus said without preamble, 'to nurse what looks like a bad case of dope. Do you think you can persuade her?'

'If it's that bad I'm sure I can,' answered Christine unhesitatingly.

'Good work, my sweet. We're worried because we can't find Craigie. If you get any word from or about him, pass it on quickly. Tell Bob, too, and the others.'

There was silence from Christine for some seconds, and then in a quieter voice she said:

'Yes, all right. Does this girl you've got know anything about him?'

'She might.'

'How much are you going to tell Marion Caroll? How far are you going to trust her?'

'Probably quite a bit,' said Loftus. 'But that's up to Bruce. Anyway we can't say much about it until she's here and knows the job that he's got in mind.'

'No—o,' said Christine. 'Has anything else happened?'

Loftus smiled into the telephone. 'Have a heart, love, we've more than enough on our hands as it is. Don't ask for more.'

'Ah, well, look after yourself,' said Christine, and rang off.

Loftus replaced the receiver and limped slowly towards an armchair.

'I gathered that Christine thinks Marion Caroll might be useful. She doesn't often guess wrong in that kind of thing. Anyhow, she seems confident that the girl will come up. Oh, damn, I didn't give her an address.'

'I'll ring her later,' said Bruce. 'She'd better come to my flat. I'll get a doctor to see Hilary Crayshaw. There's that man

Grunfelt.' He paused. 'It might be an idea to have another man's opinion first, and check Grunfelt's against it.' He moved restlessly. 'The more I think of it, the more I believe the girl's important, Bill. They did try to hang her, whatever her precious parent says, and today's attempt makes it pretty certain they didn't do it in a fit of pique. They can only want her dead because she knows something.'

Loftus waited.

'*And* she's one of those empty-headed little nit-wits who go chasing round after drugs for sensation and thinks you're a back number if you don't know the latest night-club. What the hell *can* she know?' He kicked a chair leg gloomily. 'And what had Craigie found out, or did they take him just because he's Craigie?'

'They might have done.' Loftus looked at the reports on the desk; he had been able to arrange for them to be delivered to him instead of Craigie, a comparatively simple matter since he had often worked as Craigie's chief *aide*. 'Crayshaw's recent activities have been concerned solely with the war. Ferdinand was a refugee from France in the early days of hostilities, a casino-haunting Englishman with more money than sense. He left most of his money in France. He knew the Crayshaws at Monte, told Crayshaw he was hard up, and took over the job of partnering Hilary.'

Hammond snapped: 'There's a pointer there. Ferdinand spent a lot of time in France, the breeding ground of German cosmopolitan spies. Ferdinand was hard up, was he? Supposing he'd lost his money at the tables before the war started? Supposing he was in German pay, and was sent over to keep in touch with the Crayshaws? Crayshaw would be a big prize at any time, a man always *au fait* with odds and ends of official and confidential information. Hilary's lap-dog probably had two sources of income. Emile's boot being in his flat brings that within reason.'

'Then why kill him?' objected Loftus.

'Yes, why?' asked Hammond sharply. 'Work from the assumption that Ferdinand was the spy in the Crayshaw household, and—'

He paused. Loftus said nothing, watching Hammond's restless eyes, sensing how quickly ideas were flowing in and out of the man's mind.

Hammond snapped: 'Here's why. Hilary had to be killed but Ferdinand had fallen for her. He objected to her murder, and was killed to stop him from talking. It could fit.'

Loftus said: 'Ye—es. They've been about together for some time, although you didn't get the impression that the girl was fond of him, did you?'

'What the heck does that matter? She's not fond of anyone but herself. Can't you find somebody who knew the couple personally?'

'Reports, reports,' said Loftus, riffling through the papers on the desk. He picked up one after another, many of them in code, then snapped his fingers. 'I'm crazy. I'll 'phone Miller.' He dialled Scotland Yard, and in a few seconds was speaking to the Superintendent. He put two pertinent questions, and Hammond saw that his eyes brightened while his manner grew tense.

'You're sure ... yes, of course ... good man!'

'It fits all right,' he said very gently. 'There is confirmation that Ferdinand—surname, Clay—was indeed keen on Hilary, and as jealous as they make 'em. Miller's been able to get a pretty clear picture of the association, and the evidence is that in spite of Ferdinand's faithfulness the girl didn't care a hoot for him.'

'Anything about his other friends?' Hammond asked.

'Nothing as yet that might help us,' said Loftus, impressed by Hammond's lack of cock-crowing.

Hammond lit a cigarette. 'The search for Craigie still top priority?'

'As far as it can be. Until he turns up, I'll be in the office to collate the reports. And you?'

'Getting those doctors,' said Hammond. 'I'd like a word with them in person first, particularly Grunfelt.'

He reached for his hat, but before going out the telephone rang. He paused, hearing a voice that he recognised but which held a ring of such urgency that he was startled.

'Miller here,' said Superintendent Miller. 'Where's Loftus?'

'Coming,' said Hammond, as Loftus approached him. 'What's the trouble?'

'Trouble! Muire, Cator and Uppingham were killed in Crayshaw's office this morning. Crayshaw was late for a meeting. It looks as if he just missed it.'

Hammond said quietly: 'How was it done?'

'A lung irritant poison, we don't know which one yet.'

Hammond passed over the telephone after giving Loftus the gist of what Miller had said. Loftus spoke once or twice, and then said:

'Crayshaw came here, instead of going to the meeting, I think. But wait a minute, Miller—Uppingham, Muire and Cator were ... oh, all right.'

He rang off, looking at Hammond.

'He's had to go, but you'll do as an audience instead.' He paused, and Hammond waited with no visible impatience. Then: 'The three dead men were all friends of Crayshaw's, very nearly his only friends. Were they killed because of that? Or were they killed without Crayshaw because he had Hilary on his mind, and came here?'

Hammond said slowly: 'Search me. They could have been

125

killed because they were prospective delegates to the conference, you know.' He pursed his lips, shrugged, and then said:
'We'd better let it settle down to the right level, Bill. I'm really
going for those doctors.'

When he had gone, Loftus smiled a little one-sidedly,
reflecting that Hammond reacted to new discoveries and
outrages in much the same way. He refused to be rushed into
theories, creating the impression that whatever developed was
not for the moment of great importance.

'But he'll be worrying it like a dog a bone,' Loftus said
aloud.

It was some four hours afterwards that Hammond telephoned with several matters for attention. In the first place,
Marion Caroll was in London, and Hilary was at his,
Hammond's flat. The two doctors had agreed on their opinion: Crayshaw's daughter was suffering from the effects of a
drug not yet diagnosed, and her alternative fits of hysteria and
acute depression were almost certainly due to a recent lack of
supplies.

'It looks as if she was expecting to get some from the fellow
in Hyde Park,' Hammond said. 'By the way, Grunfelt's all right.
I nearly laughed when I saw him. I'd pictured a teutonic head
and a guttural accent, but he's a three-generation Englishman.
A prominent psychiatrist as far as I can make out, and he's
treated Hilary for some eighteen months. Both he and the
other fellow say that rest and nursing will pull her round.
She's in a coma at the moment.'

'Yes?' said Loftus.

'The poison on the arrows is being checked at Scotland
Yard; it's not one of the more common ones, but we didn't
think it would be. There's nothing in the pockets of either
man to help us. Names cut out of clothes and the usual
precautions, although the suit was nearly new, and Miller is

trying to trace it. The man Eric has been identified—a young artist of the "my-worth-isn't appreciated" persuasion, very hard up until a few months ago, when he started throwing money about.' Hammond paused, and then went on quietly: 'I've just had an idea, Bill. Will you find out whether the Brice fellow at Weymouth, knew either Ferdinand Clay or this Eric Hammerton?'

'Yes,' promised Loftus promptly.

'Thanks. I think that's the lot for now. No news your end, I suppose?'

'Not a ruddy trace,' said Loftus bitterly. 'We have learned that gas was smelt near the door last night. There's not much doubt they gassed him and took him off. A car went out of the road a few minutes afterwards, but no-one knows whose it was or how many occupants were in it.'

'Where was Craigie last seen?' asked Hammond.

Loftus said: 'At Number 10, Downing Street, as far as I can find out. Hershall's personally given the order to find Craigie at all costs, and he's promised to come to the office before the day's out. Do you want to be here?'

'Not necessarily,' said Hammond, 'unless he wants to see me.'

They rang off, and in his flat Hammond turned to Marion Caroll.

The girl was standing in the threshold of the room; he could see the end of the bed behind her.

'No luck?' she said.

'Not yet,' said Hammond.

He had told her that Craigie had gone, had told her also something, although not all, of the purposes of Department Z. He had outlined the present problem, surprising himself by the freedom with which he talked. She had taken the inference quickly: first Emile, then Hilary, were in danger because they knew something of importance, and Hammond wanted to know what it was.

He had a queer feeling that she was much happier than when he had first seen her.

'She's asleep,' Marion said, 'and much quieter. It might be several hours before she wakes up. Is there anything I can do?'

Hammond said: 'Do you have to wear that uniform?'

She laughed at the unexpectedness of the question.

'It's usual, Mr. Hammond.'

'When I start being conventional I'll give up,' said Hammond, and much of the weight and anxiety in his mind faded. 'Don't tell me you haven't any other clothes with you?'

'I can't wear—'

'Yes, you can. You're working for me, and it's an order.' His eyes laughed at her. 'There's something about the uniform that absolutely prohibits me from calling you Marion!' He went on more soberly: 'I'm counting a lot on you. I'm backing a conviction that we'll get at the truth through Hilary Crayshaw and Emile. Emile's done his part, Hilary's to follow. When she comes round, she'll confide in a girl she'll have the nerve to think is her own kind, but to confide in a nurse might be less appealing.'

'All right, I'll change,' said Marion.

Hammond watched her withdraw, then leaned back with his eyes closed, letting his mind run methodically over every item reported to him or learned by him in the past forty-eight hours. Why, he wondered, had three of Crayshaw's closest friends been murdered? Was it coincidental, or was there a connection? He heard Marion return to the room, and opened his eyes.

'No, I'm not asleep,' he assured her. 'And I'd just about reached the end of the thinking process, if it is a process.' He stood up, looking at her with unfeigned interest and appreciation. 'My dear girl, it was a crime indeed to put on that sack they call a uniform!'

He had known she was lovely but had not realised how a woman's individuality could be diminished by uniformity of dress. Even her hair looked different, conscious of having shaken off an iron restriction.

She smiled, but ignored the comment.

'Any sound from the patient?' she said.

'No nothing at all.'

'I'd better have a look at her,' said Marion, and moving back to the girl's room, opened the door. Hammond, behind her, saw, almost simultaneously, the dangling legs and brightly polished black shoes.

The shoes were on a level with Marion's head, and their wearer was suspended from the ceiling.


There was a brief second of silence before Hammond snapped: 'Get behind me!' moving forward so quickly that Marion hardly realised what was happening.

She did not see the gun in his hand, and ignoring the order she leapt toward the bed, where Hilary was lying. She heard a muffled report and a gasp from somewhere near the ceiling. Another, and the gasp was repeated, while the legs and the shoes sagged drunkenly.

Hammond went forward, reaching up with his left hand and grabbing an ankle.

The man suspended from a rope coming from a hole in the ceiling was kicking in a frenzy of pain and terror. From above there was no other sound, and Hammond's fear that there might be an answering shot from the hole, which was a little more than a foot square, receded. He pocketed his gun, put his right hand to support his left, and tugged with all his strength.

The man lost his grip on the rope, and Hammond moved aside, lessening the weight of the man's fall.

He saw a short, slim man, dark-haired and olive-skinned whose yellowish eyes were wide with fear and pain. Hammond laid him full length on the floor and ran through his pockets; he found an automatic and, fastened to the left suspender, a small dagger in a sheath. He put them both in his pocket, and said quickly:

'Is she all right?'

'She seems to be,' said Marion.

'Leave her for a moment, then, and stay by the door,' said Hammond. 'Make sure the front door's locked first.' He pulled a chair into position beneath the hole in the ceiling. The hole was well-camouflaged when closed, he knew, for he had seen nothing amiss with the pattern of the ceiling paper.

He was just able to reach the sides and get a grip on the upper floor. He did not think there would be any danger.

He believed that if anyone else had been in the flat above there would have been action before this. With a couple of violent lurches he found himself in Ferdinand's unpretentious living room.

The carpet was rolled back half-way across the room. In one of the floor boards was fastened a ring to which the rope was attached. He went through the other rooms quickly, but found no one there. He went to the front door, opened it—to find himself faced with an automatic pistol held in the hand of a tall, fair-haired man.

They stared at each other in tense silence.

Then the man lowered his gun, and brushed a hand across his forehead. His expression was one of complete bewilderment.

'Hammond, you don't know how lucky you were!'

'Hallo,' said Hammond calmly.

Now he recognised the other as Carruthers, a Department agent.

'I've been on this landing for three hours,' Carruthers said, and added glumly: 'When I did think I'd got a chance of crowning someone, you turn up. The invisible man again.' He grinned, put his gun away, and went on: 'I suppose the flatfoot on the fire-escape was having a nap. You came in that way, did you?'

'No,' said Hammond, 'but presumably someone else did.' He led the way to the kitchen and the back door, from which the occupants of the flat could reach the fire-escape. He unlocked the door, and looked outside. A gruff voice said promptly: 'Stay where you are!'

Carruthers poked his head round the door. 'Hallo, Dave, so you did go to sleep.'

The plainclothes man, one of Miller's staff, regarded Carruthers in mingled surprise and annoyance. His voice, when it came, was more than injured.

'Indeed I did not, sir. I've been watching this door for the last three hours, so help me.'

Carruthers looked blankly at Hammond.

'D'you hear that?'

'Ye—es,' said Hammond slowly. He eyed the policeman, and judged him to be a man of thorough reliability.

Carruthers said: 'D'you say someone got in, Hammond?'

'I certainly do.'

'But I didn't see anyone.'

'I certainly did not,' said the policeman gruffly.

'As it's highly improbable that he floated invisibly through the air,' Hammond said reasonably, 'there must be a way in, apart from the front and back doors and the windows. Will you see what you can do about finding it?'

Carruthers drew a deep breath.

'You can't have been seeing things, I suppose?' he asked hopefully.

Hammond smiled. 'No, old man, not a chance. But I'm going to have a chat with the gentleman who evaded you. If he talks it'll save you from looking.'

14

## LITTLE MAN DOESN'T KNOW

H ow are things making out?'
'Pretty involved,' said Hammond with a shrug.
'Bad luck,' said Carruthers. 'You would pick on a business like this to start with, wouldn't you? None of it's really running to form, as far as I can gather. Bits and pieces that don't match or gel sticking out all over the place, and with Gordon taking a trip—' The flippancy of the words hid a real anxiety. 'Odd how everything always goes back to Craigie. No news, I suppose?' The last sentence was deliberately casual.

'Not yet,' admitted Hammond.

He opened the door with his key, and was stepping across the threshold when Carruthers suddenly snapped: 'Get down!'

Hammond paused in the middle of a step, and then Carruthers hooked his legs from under him, dropping to the floor at the same time. Hammond went down heavily, while Carruthers, whipping a gun from his pocket, snapped: 'Come out of there!'

Recovering himself slowly, Hammond looked up to see

Marion stepping from the bedroom. By then Carruthers was on one knee, staring dazedly towards the girl.

Hammond spoke with real irritation. 'What the devil was that for?'

Carruthers straightened up slowly. 'Er—' he said, 'I—er—thought—oh, Christmas, what is this? The flat with a hundred doors?'

Hammond rubbed his elbow ruefully, but was beginning to smile.

'It's all right, Marion, Carruthers is a bit too zealous! Let that serve for an introduction, will you?'

Carruthers beamed at Marion as he put his gun into his pocket. 'Apologies and all that,' he said brightly. 'I thought you were drawing a bead on us. Hammond didn't warn me that the most beautiful woman in London was at his flat. I can't think how he overlooked it. How do you do?'

Marion smiled gravely, as Hammond called out: 'Carruthers, come in here, will you?'

In the large bedroom, Hammond was bending over the little man on the floor, while Hilary Crayshaw lay in bed, her face chalk-white, sheets tucked up to her chin.

Carruthers took the situation in quickly, without experiencing any surprise. Surprise was not an emotion which came freely to any Department Z man.

Hammond looked up.

'Give me a hand with him,' he said. 'I'll take his legs.' Carruthers gathered his head and shoulders up gently, while Hammond contrived to raise the man's wounded leg without causing him much pain, and together they carried him into the living-room.

Marion spread a blanket on the settee, and they lowered him gently on to it.

Hammond looked down on to the recumbent figure. 'You came to shoot Miss Crayshaw, did you?'

The yellowish eyes widened, there was fear in them, but he answered promptly, as if knowing that delay would serve him no purpose.

'Y—yes.'

'Who sent you?'

'F—fryer,' muttered the little man, and gasped. 'My leg, you must get a doctor, my leg—'

'All in good time,' said Hammond, without expression in his voice. 'You came to shoot and got shot instead. A little pain will help you to remember that. Who is Fryer?'

'He—he's the Boss,' gasped the little man. 'Oo-oo my leg, I can't stand it any longer. I can't stand it!'

'Where does he live?' Hammond demanded.

'I don't know!'

'Where does Fryer live?' Hammond repeated.

'*Sacre dios*, I do not know. Have I not told you? I have never visited him, he always sends messages, he—'

'As a Spaniard, even an anglicised one,' said Hammond contemplatively, 'you know the persuasive power of pain.'

Esteven gasped: 'No, no, I cannot tell you, I will tell you everything I know of Fryer!' There were beads of sweat at his forehead and his upper lip, and the yellowish whites of his eyes showed as he strained his eyeballs upwards. 'Never have I visited Fryer, always I have seen him by appointment.'

'It would be a pity to delay calling a doctor to staunch your wound,' suggested Hammond. 'One understands that time is important in such cases.'

'It's not a lie, it is the truth!' screamed Esteven. 'Always I see him outside, always!'

Hammond said: 'Where do you meet him?'

'Mostly—mostly at the Lamplighter, the Lamplighter!'

Marion saw Hammond start. 'What is Fryer like?'

'He—he is a big man, a big man!'

'So are several hundred thousand other people in London,' said Hammond, his voice suddenly taking on a savage note. 'Don't stall, Esteven. What's he like?'

'He is big—he has black hair—he is American! Let me go, I can tell you no more. I can tell you no more!' He broke into a frenzied outburst, whilst the sweat streamed down his cheeks. 'Always I have to obey Fryer, unless I do I am killed, and always I obey. Never is it much, only once before has it been to kill. I wished to refuse, but Fryer—'

He broke off, muttering little more than an unintelligible gibberish. Hammond hesitated, and then looked round towards the door. He did not appear surprised to see Marion, but said easily: 'Will you take down what he says? There's a pad in that bureau.' He nodded towards a small writing-desk, and in a few seconds Marion was sitting at it with paper in front of her and a pencil poised.

Hammond went to Esteven: 'Stop gibbering!' The man paused, and Hammond went on: 'You've always taken Fryer's orders, no matter what they've been and they've included murder. Is that right?'

'Yes, yes, please fetch the doctor quickly. I have killed, I killed Ferdinand, I killed him!' He was writhing, not in pain but in mental agony.

Hammond's heart leapt, and he paused only long enough to give Marion time to write down the confession. Then he asked: 'Did you try to hang the girl?'

'I—I was forced to, Fryer was with me, there were others, I could not help myself!'

'That's too bad,' said Hammond.

He asked a dozen questions, and the answers came with varying degrees of reluctance; the important thing was that they came. Esteven admitted that he and Fryer and another man he had known as 'Patsy' had been at the Lamplighter on the night of the attack on Ferdinand and Hilary Crayshaw. They had come from the club to Ferdinand's flat, where Hilary, quite drunk, had started to dance, taking off her shoes and stockings. But for Ferdinand's restraining influence she would have stripped herself completely; it had happened that way before, Esteven said.

Then the girl had collapsed, and Fryer had taken something from her bag; what it was Esteven swore that he did not know, and Hammond did not think the man would lie in that one non-essential while telling so much that damned him. Fryer had then announced that the girl was to be killed. Ferdinand, who worked with Fryer on matters of which Esteven had little knowledge, had strongly, even violently, opposed this. After some argument, Fryer had appeared to give way. He had left the flat, but later returned. Between them Esteven continued, Ferdinand had been overpowered and strangled; the girl had been lowered into his, Hammond's flat, and Esteven had followed. He had carried out Fryer's instructions implicitly, and strung the girl up behind the door.

The next day Fryer had told him that the girl was not dead. Hammond gathered that her recovery had been used as a threat to make Esteven even more acquiescent in whatever Fryer wanted; it was easy to see that the little man had been terrorised.

On the failure of a second attempt, Esteven had received instructions to try yet again; and in fear of his life, he obeyed.

'How did you get upstairs?' Hammond asked.

'There is—a fanlight,' Esteven gasped. 'It is blackened but it is there, leading from the loft. To reach the roof from the next-door house is easy; I am small and quick to move. I came in that way.'

Carruthers grimaced, and muttered:

'The simple explanation. Who'd think of a fanlight, when he could conjure up an invisible man?'

'It doesn't matter,' said Hammond. 'In fact it was as well, I think. That'll do fine, Marion. Will you 'phone for a doctor—what's the name of the Department's man, Carruthers?'

'Doc Little,' said Carruthers, and gave Marion the doctor's number.

By then Esteven was lying still on the settee. There was no movement except for a shiver which convulsed his whole body from time to time.

Hammond did not think that the man would be in a condition to talk further; and he had said enough. Hammond stepped to the bureau and glanced through Marion's notes. He was still pondering over them when a man of enormous girth, a little out of breath from mounting the stairs, entered the flat and was introduced by Carruthers as Doc Little, once an active agent of the Department. He examined the wounded leg, pulled at his pendulous under-lip, suggested an ambulance and a nursing-home; within half-an-hour both Esteven and the doctor had gone.

Carruthers, at Hammond's suggestion, went with them: there was always a chance that the man would know more.

Hammond lit a cigarette and sat back in an easy chair; Marion thought that she had rarely known a man who could relax so completely; she remembered the speed of his earlier movements, and the decisiveness of his method with Esteven, almost as if it were something she had experienced in a dream. About Hammond's rather dreamy face there was no hint that he could act with such force and ruthlessness. She was aware then, of the strength and character in the man; but she saw further than that. He had done what he had, because he knew the desperate need for it. He was working for a cause; it was part of him, a dangerous part, and he would let nothing stand in the way of its triumph.

She felt as if she had known Bruce Hammond for a long time.

He looked up as she came out of the bedroom. 'How is she?'

'Still asleep.'

'Good. It must be some sleep, but it's as well. Quite a little lady, isn't she?'

'The chief cause of that must lie at the door of the one who first gave her the drugs.'

'Ye—es. That's so. Do you always look for the cause before the effect?'

'It's the sensible thing to do.'

'I can see you're right,' mused Hammond. 'The effect of this whole shindy is pretty obvious, but the cause of it is what we're after. However, I think we're nearer. Fryer and the Lamplighter together should give us something, and we'd better try the place tonight.' He paused. 'What's the time?'

'Ten past four,' she said, glancing at her wrist watch.

'I wonder if there's anything in the way of food in the larder?' asked Hammond.

'I'll find out.'

'We'll find out,' he amended.

There were no biscuits, but there was bread, butter, jam and a small tin of sardines. They carried everything on a tray into the living room, where they sat opposite each other. Marion poured out while Hammond, suddenly dropping the half-humorous banter in which he had been indulging in the kitchen, said quietly:

'The thing Fryer took from the bag might or might not have been the gold cross.' He frowned. 'You don't know much about that but you'll learn. Whatever it was, it frightened her

139

out of her wits. Her father behaved very differently from the way she had expected,' he added slowly, and stopped abruptly.

An atmosphere had sprung into the room, something entirely new, inspired by his words and the way in which they were uttered. He was looking at her intently, and yet she did not think he was seeing her.

'Very differently from the way she had expected,' he repeated *sotto voce*. 'The key-words to the whole problem, I think. I wonder if it's possible—'

He broke off. Marion made no comment. He looked at her with a one-sided smile.

'You're good, Marion, too good in some ways! Not a single "What the hell are you talking about?" '

'I could ask questions,' Marion said dryly.

'No, don't!' He broke in hastily. 'Just go on as you are doing. I've a fixation,' he added, this time looking into her eyes and undoubtedly seeing her '—about questions and answers and ideas. If I get an idea and share it, I react badly to the chance that the other fellow thinks it's balderdash. Often it is,' he added with a grin. 'Can you put up with me?'

'I'll do my best.'

Hammond said ruefully, 'You're laughing at me. There's nothing like a woman to make a man feel his own unimportance. However, I think we're getting places. We've solved several of the minor problems, and we can now move forward towards the next objective—the Lamplighter.'

'You seem to know it.'

'Yes, Hilary mentioned it as a night club. Quite the latest thing. You've been Rip van Winkling if you don't know it.' His eyes smiled at her. 'I think it would be an idea if you and I went along for an hour or two this evening.'

He prepared to take her acceptance for granted, and passed his cup. 'Is there another? ... thanks.'

The front door bell rang sharply.

'I'll go,' said Marion.

She was better placed, for to get up he had to move a table. He watched her walk across the room and open the hall door, and then heard her explain. He was up and round the table within seconds; then he saw Loftus.

Half-hidden by Marion, Hammond saw a shorter man than Loftus, with bull-like shoulders and a pale round face. He knew at once why Marion was startled; he was nearly as startled himself to see the Prime Minister walk towards him.

## 15

## WHAT CRAIGIE KNEW

Hammond's expression grew blank; he neither smiled nor frowned, but waited for Loftus. Hammond was aware of the intent gaze from Hershall's eyes, felt that the Prime Minister was trying to assess his value and his worth.

Then Loftus said: 'This is Hammond, sir.'

Hershall nodded.

'You're having quite a time of it, I'm told,' he said easily. 'Is there any tea in that pot? Loftus made me miss mine.' He smiled, and Hammond's tension relaxed. Here was a man who might ask for impossibilities and often get them done, but who would remain human and understanding.

Hammond looked at Marion.

'There's a kettle on,' she said.

Hershall turned his head towards her, as Hammond murmured an introduction.

'Excellent! I feel like bartering half my kingdom for a cup of tea at the moment!' He smiled warmly as she hurried to the kitchen.

Hershall turned abruptly. 'I wanted to see you, Hammond.

THE DAY OF DISASTER

Loftus has told me all there is to know about you, or all he knows.' The keen eyes twinkled. 'Anyhow, I like what I can see, and you'll want to hear this. Go on, Loftus.'

'Craigie saw Mr. Hershall late last night, Bruce. There were two things that he learned—first, that you were right about the manoeuvres; they're due on or about the twenty-first.'

Hammond nodded.

'The other is a conference of some importance, which—'

Hershall snorted: 'Some importance! Infernal understatement, Loftus; it's of immense importance. I see I'd better do the telling.' Quickly, without a word wasted, he outlined what he had said to Craigie, adding the names of the men whom he expected to be at the conference, and that it was not yet decided whether Crayshaw's Dorset home or Cavendish's Hertfordshire one was to be used.

'And what of Muire, Uppingham and Cator?' asked Hammond.

Hershall said: 'Cator is a serious loss. I wasn't too satisfied with the others, but Cator and Crayshaw between them were going to get them into action on the scale I want. Crayshaw will be badly upset. They were practically his only friends, and the friendship was based as much on business as anything else. They're all in engine manufacture, but you'd know that.'

'Would you mind telling me just how close your friendship is with Crayshaw?' asked Hammond.

Hershall eyed him narrowly.

'Ye—es. I've been waiting for that. Not a talkative nor a demonstrative man, Crayshaw, but at my suggestion he had plans for converting his factories to war output, had large quantities of machinery on the stocks to get into operation as soon as war started. He is a man that I can rely on, but whom I could never get close to—d'you follow me? He was the same, even as a boy. I haven't seen much of him lately—'

'What does "lately" mean, exactly?' asked Hammond.

'The past month or so,' answered Hershall.

As he spoke Marion came in with a fresh pot of tea. The Prime Minister watched her as she poured out, accepted a cup with a smile, and turned to Hammond.

'Well?' asked Hershall abruptly.

'Well,' said Hammond, speaking with the hesitancy of one measuring his words, 'we have to face up to it.'

'Face up to what?' barked Hershall.

'If Craigie was kidnapped because he'd been to see you, the kidnappers knew he'd made the visit, and more or less what you had told him.'

'Now, come,' said Hershall a trifle impatiently. 'What did they think? That as Craigie was taken off I wouldn't tell his assistants?'

Hammond said doggedly, 'I don't think you've quite followed my reasoning, sir. When did you tell Loftus?'

'An hour ago, I suppose.' Hershall paused, and then went on quickly: 'All right, I see what you mean. It caused a delay of fourteen or fifteen hours.'

'Yes,' said Hammond. 'The delay was important; they wanted to do something during that time. Has anything been done to your knowledge?'

'Go on, go on,' said Hershall. 'What do you mean?'

'Have you made any arrangments in the last twelve hours?' asked Hammond. 'About the manoeuvres, or the venue of the conference?'

'No,' said Hershall.

'That's queer,' mused Hammond. 'I would have thought— but it doesn't matter, sir. I could never collect thoughts as quickly as I'd like to! You might be interested to know what has happened here,' he added, and looked at Marion again: 'Have you got your notes?'

Hershall looked through them with keen interest.

'Hm. Precious young woman, Miss Crayshaw.'

'Very much so,' said Hammond wryly. 'We'll have to make sure that she's not harmed.'

'We'll have to warn Crayshaw, although the Throgmorton Street crime will put him on the alert,' said Hershall. 'Of course—' he paused, tapping his thumb against his saucer, 'I knew about his difficulties with Hilary. Felt very sorry for him. Children are always an anxiety, but she's been rather more than that.' He stopped tapping, and snapped: 'You haven't any direct suspicion of Crayshaw, have you?'

'If the circumstances asked for it, I would suspect you,' said Hammond quietly.

'Hmm,' said Hershall. 'I'm not going to tell you your business, Hammond, but Crayshaw—' he paused. 'We've been life-long friends, a thing to remember. No man has put more into the war effort; haven't a better war-horse in the country. The man's produced prodigious results, prodigious. You should know that.'

'I had an idea,' admitted Hammond with a smile. 'But he's concerned somehow, sir. The man Ferdinand was planted on him, his daughter was deliberately induced to take drugs; she might well have helped Ferdinand to get information. I'd say that it was likely that most of the Crayshaw production figures have reached Berlin, piecemeal, if not *en masse*.'

'Uncomfortable thought,' said Hershall, 'but not necessarily convincing, and even if it were, they were not a vital secret. Total production would not be known.'

'No,' said Hammond quickly, 'but total production, past, present and prospective, will probably be discussed at the conference?'

'It will,' said Hershall. He stood up abruptly.

'There's no point in my staying longer,' he said. 'Don't get

145

up, Loftus! Both of you know that I'm expecting results, and I don't mind how you get them.' He paused, to give added weight to those words. 'The only thing I shall mind is if I don't. Good luck, Hammond.'

Hammond preceded him to the door.

In the hall the two special branch men, who followed the Prime Minister everywhere, fell into line. Hershall started to go out, then turned and put his head inside the hall again. 'Goodbye, Miss Caroll. Don't let them overwhelm you!' He chuckled and went downstairs quickly and surely; a few moments later the front door of the house slammed.

Hammond turned slowly back into the room.

Loftus was talking to Marion. He looked up quickly. 'Well, Bruce, what did you think of him?'

Hammond smiled. 'A bit tempestuous,' he said, 'but he's damned smart. He picked up my Crayshaw angle almost before I picked it up myself. However, that will work itself out.' He whistled tunelessly under his breath, and then added: 'I wonder what happened during the night?'

'You could be backing a wrong hunch,' said Loftus.

Hammond turned to Marion in mock-exasperation.

'That's just what I was saying. The only safe thing is to keep one's thoughts to oneself!' He looked back at Loftus. 'I shall like that remark a lot less if it's true, Bill. Now, what have you got for me?'

Loftus pursed his lips.

'We—ell, not a great deal. The commissionaire remains missing. There's no sign of Craigie. Crayshaw had been at his office all day. You've worked out the Ferdinand angle yourself, but we would have got there—we found a box of book matches in the pocket of the archer; it was from the Lamplighter, an advertising packet. Brice visited the Lamplighter, when he was in London. Reports from Dorset don't give us much more information than we've got, except further proof that the radio-car which went after Brice last night had no right to, although if we hadn't raised the point probably no one would have thought anything of it.' He paused. 'Emile's much better; Lois and Christine are looking after him, and the place is guarded so well that there's nothing to fear there. Our immediate problem seems to be to make sure that Hilary's safe.'

'And discover what it was she lost,' Hammond said.

Marion spoke into a pause: 'The P.M. seemed to know all about her.'

'Oh, Crayshaw's story was quite genuine,' said Loftus. 'Sorry, Bruce, but there's no doubt about it. We've even seen people who found the gold cross when it's been lost before, and who claimed the reward for it. The only point outstanding is the whereabouts of her shoes and stockings.'

'Ye—es,' said Hammond. 'And why the handbag was in the larder. I wonder—' he turned abruptly and without another word went into the kitchen. The others heard the movements of crockery and of tins, then a comparative silence, followed by Hammond's footsteps. When he reached the living room again he had a pair of stockings over one arm, and was carrying some shoes.

Marion and Loftus stared at them blankly.

'And so that's another mystery busted,' said Hammond. 'Except that I can't see why the stuff was in the larder ... Unless they foraged in there for something to eat, and thought it as good a place as any to leave the oddments.' He sighed. 'Well, if we don't make the progress we'd like on the big matters, we're getting the odds and ends nicely cleared up. What about arrangements for the Lamplighter?' he added.

'What have you in mind?' asked Loftus.

'A raid, of course, if Fryer's there. We mustn't let him get

147

away. He might not talk as easily as Esteven, but at least he'll be in jug instead of running about and doing more harm. Once we've got him too, we can check on his recent movements.'

'I'll tell half a dozen of the boys to be at the Lamplighter tonight,' said Loftus, 'and we'll have to leave the outside arrangements to the police. I'll 'phone you about it. You've seen the photographs of the agents you haven't yet met?'

'Yes, I won't crown the wrong man,' promised Hammond.

'You're a matter-of-fact blighter,' Loftus said with appreciation. 'If only we could get Craigie back he'd enjoy hearing and seeing you. Well, I'm off to the office.'

'What are we going to do with Hilary?' asked Marion.

'I'll send the Errols for her,' promised Loftus. 'I know just the place.'

From a window in the living room they watched him walk slowly across the road to a waiting cab. Also by the cab was a tall, grey-clad man, who even from that distance looked tired and even weary.

'Who's that?' asked Marion.

'By name, Davidson,' said Hammond. 'Wally Davidson. I'm told he's been in hospital more times than any other of Craigie's men.' He was smiling a little, but the smile slowly disappeared. 'Loftus is a grand chap,' he said. 'He's right on top of himself now, although Craigie told me that at one time it looked as if losing his leg would finish him for all general work. He was engaged, you know. American girl. She was killed in one of the show-downs, and Christine pulled him through. Loftus hasn't yet convinced himself that Christine's interest is more than pity skilfully disguised. Odd fellow in some ways.'

Marion said: 'Most of those I've met recently are. You don't really think about anything else than the Department, do you? You live in it and for it?'

Hammond eyed her with a curious smile.

'Ye—es, I suppose it looks like that. And it's true enough that my biggest concern at the moment is Crayshaw. It looks as if he's going to be a real stumbling block. The P.M. loves him as a brother.'

'The P.M. told you to get results, and that he didn't mind how you got them,' Marion reminded him. 'I think he was telling you not to pay any attention to anything he said, but to work on whatever lines you think are the right ones.'

Hammond said: 'Did you think that, too? All the same, Crayshaw—' he paused, and went into a brief brooding mood, rocking a little on his heels. Then: 'He didn't act as Hilary expected, did he?'

'Why is that so important?'

'We—ell, he might not act, now, as other people expect,' said Hammond. 'Also, the other side want his daughter killed. They also killed Ferdinand, which might or might not have been because of his ardent defence of Hilary. I have a feeling that his usefulness was over. There's a tie-up—can you see it?'

'No,' said Marion eagerly. 'Tell me.'

Hammond shook his head, laughing. 'You know my methods.'

'Won't you even tell me what you're going to do now?'

'As soon as Hilary's safely removed,' said Hammond, 'I'm going for a breath of fresh air, and you're coming with me. We might even have dinner out. A little relaxation will do us the world of good.'

Marion said curiously: 'Do you relax?'

Hammond laughed. 'Well, that's what I propose to do.' And then more sharply: 'I wish I knew what had happened last night.'

Marion said nothing, but went in to see her patient.

Even in sleep the spoiled, almost petulant expression was on Hilary's face. She was clearly a girl who had lacked the proper parental control, and had far too much money at hand. It was growing obvious, too, that unwittingly she had been drawn into a web of intrigue, and that she had been used to get information from her father.

Hammond was thinking along the same lines when the telephone rang.

He stepped towards it, and heard Loftus's voice a moment later, charged with unusual excitement.

'Bruce ... hold on a moment.' Hammond waited, while Marion came into the room. 'Hallo ... Bruce, you unholy beggar, how did you know?'

'I didn't know,' said Hammond. 'What's happened? Has something developed during the night?'

'Yes. What did you expect?'

'As a long shot,' said Hammond quietly, 'I expected a decision to be made about whether the conference should be held at Crayshaw's place or Cavendish's. Hershall disappointed me when he said that no decision had been reached. Well?'

'Virtually it's been reached,' said Loftus. 'Cavendish Hall was practically gutted by fire last night. There isn't a room left large enough for half a dozen people to meet, let alone a conference.'


Marion, looking into Hammond's gay eyes, knew that there was a fierce exultation in his mind. From the moment he had heard from Loftus, all depression had vanished. He had joked with the Errols when, with an ambulance and stretcher-bearers, they had come for Hilary. He had inquired light-heartedly into the arrangements for protecting Crayshaw's daughter, and had pointed out to Marion with positive gaiety the two escorting cars.

He had telephoned for a table at the Regal Hotel where, since the bombing of London had started, dinner began at half-past six, and there was dancing from seven o'clock until nine.

Now they were sitting opposite each other at a table in the large restaurant, with a crowd of people about them differing from peace-time only in so much as evening gowns and dinner jackets had given way to lounge suits and uniforms.

The orchestra was good; Hammond danced well, and Marion felt herself swept up in a vortex of gaiety and happiness she had thought she would never know again.

They returned from a waltz to find a note on Hammond's plate. He frowned at it before he opened it, but his eyes were still alight with high spirits. Turning it over, he saw in pencil the last three letters of his name: D-n-o.

He slit the envelope with the back of a knife; two tickets fell out, and a slip of paper. He glanced at the paper and read:

'These will get you into the Lamplighter.'

'Club membership cards,' he said, passing one of them to Marion. 'The Lamplighter is careful of its clientele, but not quite careful enough. Are you looking forward to the show?'

'Aren't you?'

'We're talking about you.'

'But thinking about something very different. Bruce, what is it?'

He almost brushed her hair with his lips as he whispered:

'Cavendish's place was burned down—why? Because the other alternative was Crayshaw's. I was quite sure they meant it to take place at Crayshaw's headquarters. That was why I wanted Hershall to go there. With all the members of the conference,' he added. 'It won't work out unless he does. They thought that by holding Craigie it would stop any investigation by the Department of Cavendish's place.'

'And what will happen to Craigie?'

She wished she had not asked the question, for the smile left his eyes, and he looked solemn, even sombre, as he said abruptly:

'God knows. He won't have much chance, I'm afraid. I—hallo, there's Loftus.'

He stopped talking as he looked at the big man.

Loftus was not alone; the Errols were with him, and both Hammond and Marion knew from the expressions on the faces of the three men that the news they brought was bad. Loftus picked his way carefully through the crowded dining room, while a waiter hurried forward to arrange an extra table next to Hammond's.

For a moment nobody said anything, then Loftus's words came very slowly: 'Bruce, I don't know how this is going to affect your plans and plotting. But I do know it's knocked most of us flat. There were two people killed at Cavendish's place last night. One was burned beyond recognition, the other burned badly about the head and shoulders, but with his coat in one piece.'

Hammond said in a strained voice: 'Well?'

'In the coat was Craigie's wallet,' said Loftus. 'I'm flying down to identify the body right away.'

'Oh!' said Hammond. His hand pressed on the table so that the knuckles showed white. 'Cavendish's place. You think they took Craigie there?'

'It makes a hash of your ideas about Crayshaw,' said Mark Errol abruptly.

# 16

# THE LAMPLIGHTER

Paying no attention to Mark, Hammond looked straight at Loftus. 'You can't be sure that it's Craigie. Why was the top of the body burned and not the torso? Accident, or design?'

'That's what I'm wondering,' said Loftus, 'and I'm praying that it was design.'

'But why should they want to make it look as if Craigie were dead?' demanded Mike Errol.

'It looks pretty senseless to me,' Mark said.

Hammond snapped: 'For heaven's sake use your brain, man. Craigie, or the death of Craigie, at Cavendish Hall would be a prime bait for us. They would reason that the men they've most to fear in the Department would hurry down there. The whole venue of operations would alter, and that's what they want. The place went up in flames to make a beacon we couldn't miss. If they have their way we'll fly to it like moths about a candle. It's the counter-attraction, the thing to get us away.'

Loftus said evenly: 'It could be.'

'It is,' Hammond said with furious conviction. 'We can't play with "could-be's" or "might-be's" any longer.' He hesitated and then went on more slowly: 'It's only my guess, of course, until Bill brings us proof. Isn't that so, Bill?'

'As I said, I've arranged for a 'plane,' said Loftus.

'Good man, but I could use the Errols.'

Loftus said: 'You're still going to the Lamplighter?'

'Of course. They want to keep us away from there, that's quite obvious.' He pushed his chair back irritably. 'Bill, I've rather let my tongue run away with me—'

'Don't be an ass,' said Loftus. 'I won't be any good in a shindy, and I may as well go up to Cavendish Hall.'

He moved towards the door, Hammond with him, leaving the others at the table. 'Just one thing, Bruce.'

'Hm-hm?'

'Ought you to take the girl there tonight?'

Hammond said: 'I have wondered, but on the whole I think yes. I've a hunch she will be useful.'

'Your hunches!' growled Loftus, but his eyes were a little brighter. 'The odd thing is, they work.'

'Have a good journey,' said Hammond. 'I'm not really worried about the body being Craigie's.'

'I hope to God you're right,' said Loftus fervently. 'Now that the shock's over, I'm inclined to agree with you. But whose is it?'

'There's no reason why the body should be that of anyone we know, but I could guess at one who wouldn't surprise me.' Hammond shook his head in answer to Loftus's inquiring glance. 'No, I'm keeping that idea to myself.'

'Have I all the clues?' asked Loftus.

'Just as many as I have,' said Hammond. 'Happy landing!'

He watched Loftus enter the waiting taxi, and saw the car behind it; he did not recognise the man at the wheel until he climbed from the car. It was the tall and languorous Wally Davidson.

Hammond turned back into the Regal. His high spirits had gone, but his confidence was in no way affected.

The Lamplighter scoffed at war, morals, the law, and convention. It had, indeed, the same rather dreary mixture of gaiety, weariness and decadence that permeates most third-rate night clubs.

The too-high note of a girl's hysterical laughter set the standard of the club. There was nothing soft or mellow about it. The band was made up of Negroes and half-breeds, amongst them an Eurasian with a yellowish skin, who beat the drums with the peculiar intensity of a drug addict. The light, coming from the tops of the lamp-posts, which made up the greater part of the decor, was brilliant enough to hurt the eyes. It made most of the women present look ravaged and over-painted.

Marion took in the scene with contemplative eyes. Hammond leaned towards her. 'What do you make of it?'

She shrugged.

'I used to think places like this spelt adventure,' she said.

'You might have been right at that.'

'The real thing is never as romantic as the imagined,' she said, a little wistfully. 'Are your men here?'

'Some of them,' said Hammond. 'Zero hour is nine-fifteen, and it's hardly nine yet. They had to get feminine companions you know.'

Marion said: 'Do you mean they had to contact pick-ups and bring them here?'

'Just that,' he assured her.

She was silent for a moment, and then said: 'It makes a

queer story. Neither you nor Loftus, nor Kerr for that matter, would enjoy it.'

Hammond shrugged. 'A job's a job. There's no place for squeamishness in the Department.'

Marion said quietly: 'Bruce, tell me one thing.'

'Well?'

'Why did you bring me here?'

'Didn't you want to come?'

'Yes, but that's begging the question.'

'I'm not sure that I oughtn't to let it pass at that,' he said slowly. 'There was a reason, of course. Not one that you might appreciate, Marion. It's not one I appreciate all that much myself.'

'Go on,' she said. 'I can take it.'

'Well, here it comes! You're not an average type. In a joint like this you're unusual, you attract attention. If Fryer is here, or any of his men, you'll be noticed. On my own, I might not be, and if I had a lady-for-the-evening I wouldn't be. I want to attract Fryer's attention. In short, you're my bait for the evening.' He was smiling, but did not look amused. 'Does it sting?'

'Sting?' she said, and laughed at him. 'Why should it? Your methods are not unknown to me. I'm glad there's a chance that I can help, I'm glad—' she paused.

'Don't overdo it,' said Hammond. 'That's fine.'

They did not try to dance, but picked at *hors d'oeuvres* brought to them by an over-painted, over-dyed woman with an air of improbable youth. A small boy, little more than a child, offered them cigarettes and chocolates at ten times their normal price.

'And the amazing thing is that they're selling fast,' said Marion. She sounded a little dazed.

'They're living in a dream world,' said Hammond. 'The real

one is too difficult for them, so they've built another of fantasy. But you were right, Marion, it's the cause that matters not the effect. These poor beggars want sympathy and treatment, but—'

'Yessir?' piped the boy.

'I'll have twenty of these,' said Hammond, touching a packet of cigarettes.

'Yessir,' the boy handed one over, and Hammond gave him a pound note. The boy waited, without trying to find change.

'What's the trouble?'

'Another ten shillings, please, sir.' Hammond paid up, and then asked for some chocolates; again he touched a box in a corner away from the others, and the boy said: 'Fifty shillings, sir, please.'

Hammond paid; Marion formed a protest with her lips but did not utter it, for Hammond's expression forbade comment. He opened the packet of cigarettes, took out one of the little white cylinders and, instead of putting it to his lips, tapped it on the side of his plate.

A fine white powder followed a few shreds of tobacco.

Hammond said in a tense voice: 'My God, cocaine as easy as that! Why the hell aren't the police watching the place?'

'Are—are you sure?' Marion spoke with an effort.

'Even these people wouldn't have the nerve to charge those prices for normal cigarettes and chocolates. It's the effrontery of it that beats me. I think,' he added, 'you'd better open your box and pretend to eat a chocolate, but don't swallow it. I don't want you shedding clothes and doing fan dances.'

He was watching the door, which had opened to admit a party of four; he recognised the Errols with two ladies they certainly had not known before that night. They made for a corner table, and he felt satisfied; every vantage point was now represented by an agent.

Nothing else happened.

The wild cacophony of hot rhythm, harsh laughter, raised voices and clinking glasses went on without cessation, in a gradually increasing tempo. The din was almost deafening. Near them a party of eight or nine, each egging the other on, was screaming in hoarse monotony.

Suddenly Marion saw Hammond's lips tighten, his expression go blank. A colossal man in a light grey suit had entered the room. With Esteven's description in mind, it was impossible not to recognise him. Without appearing to look, Marion saw Fryer thread his way amongst the tables, a tall graceful woman by his side.

Marion said: 'What happens now?'

'I don't quite know,' said Hammond. 'To a certain extent we must play it by instinct. We'll see who visits his table, and how quickly he shows any particular interest in ours.'

Waiting, Marion noticed that already a marked deterioration was apparent in those around her. Masks were off, and few, now, were even trying to keep up a pretence of normality. The glassy eyes, the strident voices, the more than occasional obscenities, all combined to create that effect. It was easy to imagine Hilary Crayshaw dancing wildly at the Lamplighter, easy to imagine her in such a mood, throwing all discretion, all decency to the winds.

On the crowded dance floor the dancing had changed subtly.

Hammond looked at Marion's pale face.

'It's not good,' he said. 'I half wish—'

He stopped abruptly.

He saw Fryer stand up and push his chair back. The tall woman with him appeared not to notice that he was leaving the table. Fryer walked about the crowded dance floor and then approached Hammond's table near the middle of the room. No one appeared to watch him. Hammond had no doubt that each Department Z man there knew precisely how long it would take to get a gun out and, if necessary, shoot.

Marion knew that Hammond was talking with easy flippancy to create the impression he wished to create. She answered lightly, gaily, feeling beneath the sophisticated pleasantries, Hammond's increasing tension. It was an ordeal to sit there laughing, without once turning her head to see who was coming and what was happening. The band had now taken up a rhythmical chanting to which the diners were beating time with knives, glasses and plates.

Hammond saw Fryer drawing nearer. The eyes behind large glasses were dark, the big face was expressionless.

Hammond looked up; the stare from the man was so direct and deliberate that it was absurd to pretend not to notice it.

The man drew near the table; Marion too, judged the time right to turn and look at him.

Fryer reached the table and stood looking into Hammond's eyes. As a waiter hurried up with a chair, Fryer spoke in a low-pitched voice with a slight American accent: 'May I sit down?'

'I don't see why,' said Hammond easily.

'You will.' Fryer pulled the chair up, and rested his elbows lightly on the table.

'In that case,' Hammond said, 'the quicker the better.'

Fryer said deliberately: 'Mr. Hammond, I've wanted a word with you for quite a while.'

'So?'

'Since Esteven squealed,' Fryer said, in the reasonable voice of one discussing everyday matters, 'I have expected you and the boys.'

'Very natural.'

Fryer shifted the cigar he was smoking from one side of his mouth to the other.

'Your move,' Hammond murmured pleasantly.

'Sure, Hammond, sure. As you say, it's my move, and that is when it suits me. Now, if you'll forgive my mentioning it, this isn't a place to bring a nice girl like Miss Caroll; maybe you didn't think of that? I'll tell you what I'll do, Hammond, I'll give you a break. You don't deserve it, but I'll give you one.'

'Sounds delightful,' said Hammond, with real interest. 'Let's hear about it.'

'Sure. Listen now, I'll let you and all your little boys go out without a Luger bullet amongst them, and I'll let you and Miss Caroll do the same. That's all I've got to say.'

'Not quite,' said Hammond, looking at the end of his cigarette, 'you may as well finish the proposition.'

'If you will have it,' said Fryer, 'then tell the police to lay off this joint; it's profitable to me. Now listen, don't start shouting "no". You haven't a chance. This mob of dopes will do what I tell them. If I shout "raid" they'll rush the doors, and none of you can get out. See those ventilator slits?' he added, motioning towards the ceiling. 'It'll make it easier for you to decide if I tell you there's a tommy-gun on the other side of each one. Now what about paying your check and scramming?'

# 1 7
# FULL VALUE

Hammond looked down at the end of his cigarette.
The ceaseless beating of the drums and the wails of
the saxophones sent wave after wave of weird oscillations
against Hammond's ears. If here and there a man or a woman
looked disgusted, apprehensive, or worried, they made no
more than five per cent of the total gathering.

Marion found the monotonous rhythm oppressive. It
prevented her from thinking clearly, made her want to press
her hands against her temples, to jump up and run from the
room.

Instead she looked up at Hammond.

It was impossible to judge what he would do, whether he
would tacitly admit that, for the moment, Fryer had bested
him. Marion wondered fleetingly whether he had dreamed
that any ultimatum like this would be presented; and then she
remembered that he had expected to be seen and recognised,
had even brought her with him to make sure that he was
noticed; this could not be a complete surprise.

'Don't take too long thinking,' Fryer said.

Hammond looked up from his cigarette. His lips were curved as if he were amused, and his hands were quite steady.

'Fryer,' he said deliberately, 'I'm not paying my check until I've had full value. This joint makes a good profit for you, you tell me. After tonight, it won't. Did you know that Esteven had named you as Ferdinand's murderer?'

Fryer did not bat an eyelid.

'You believe him?'

'That question is hardly relevant. The point is, will twelve good men and true believe him?'

Hammond turned a mildly inquisitive gaze towards the ventilators. 'You've eight slits, which, mathematically speaking, should add up to their equivalent in guns. Quite a party, Fryer.'

Fryer snapped: 'You'll find out. Stop stalling, and give me your answer.'

Marion saw that Fryer, possessed of a massive confidence when he had reached the table, was getting shaky; it could only be because he could not understand the assurance of Hammond's manner.

'Fryer,' said Hammond gently, 'you make me tired. You're through. You were through the moment you came here tonight. If you had one tenth of the sense you think you have, you'd have kept away. But the Lamplighter was too valuable, wasn't it? A profit-maker, and a good rendezvous.'

Fryer half-rose. Hammond put out a hand and gripped the man's wrist.

'You're covered from every corner!' snapped Fryer. 'Take your mitt off me!'

'You also are covered,' murmured Hammond. 'Quite a number of my boy-friends came along tonight, but they didn't do what I did. They didn't bring a companion so obviously new to the place that they couldn't be missed. Marion—' he put his free hand to his pocket, while for Marion the tension grew almost unbearable. Hammond pulled out a wallet, keeping a steel-like grip on Fryer's right wrist. 'In the buff envelope there are photographs.' He waited while she took them out. 'You will find all the originals sitting round the edge of the room,' he went on. 'Tell them about the ventilation holes, and Fryer's idea of making the crowd mob the doors, will you?'

Fryer snarled: 'Keep where you are, you little—'

Hammond twisted his wrist; whatever epithet was intended died on Fryer's lips, while Marion pushed her chair back, and, a little dazedly, moved away, gliding from table to table, while the mad medley continued.

She felt that eyes were watching her from the ceiling.

She believed Fryer when he said that the men there held tommy-guns. She did not know how her legs carried her round the room, although she delivered her message without interruption, wondering how long her immunity would last.

Once or twice she looked towards Hammond and Fryer, still facing each other across the table.

Fryer said thickly: 'Hammond, you don't know what you're doing. Let me go!'

'I'm cleaning up the Lamplighter,' said Hammond lightly. 'But that's only a preliminary, after that there's another little matter to settle. If you try to move your wrists any more,' he added contemplatively, 'your arm will break. Bones have a peculiar reluctance to be twisted beyond a certain point.' There was sweat on Fryer's forehead, and his upper lip.

Hammond added: 'She'll be back in a moment, Fryer. When are you doing something about it?'

Fryer said nothing, while Marion neared the table, and heard Hammond go on:

'It couldn't be because you know quite well if the tommy-guns go into action they'll get you as well as me, could it? You made a mistake there, you know, but I expected it. You couldn't very well do anything else. If you'd just shot the party up without trying to get me out, nothing would have stopped the police from acting, and keeping the place surrounded. There would have been no way out.'

Fryer said thickly: 'You're right about there being no no way out—for you.'

Hammond shrugged.

'Marion, how quickly can you put on your gas-mask?'

Marion stared at him blankly.

'I'm serious,' he said, while Fryer gasped as he tried to free himself, but failed. Marion picked up her Civil Duty respirator, and glanced across the room.

The Errols were doing the same.

She began to put it on, and Hammond's voice came dully to her ears.

'You see, Fryer, you gave us safe conduct by coming here; the tommy-gun merchants just can't do a thing, in case they shoot you.' He half-rose from his chair, and then Marion saw his free hand draw back, the fist clenched.

He drove it towards Fryer's chin. There was a dull thud, as the fist met the point of Fryer's jaw. Fryer went sprawling backward, his chair crashing to the floor. There was a scream from nearby, but the orchestra went on playing, only too used to the flare-up of violence and collapse; a mêlée was not likely to attract much attention.

Hammond turned sharply to Marion: 'Get down on the floor!'

She obeyed, automatically, crouching below the clouds of gas that were rising towards the ventilators. Shrieks and oaths filled the room as the gas began to take effect.

Hammond was by her side, saying: 'Tear-gas, it's all right.'

164

She realised that the crowd was milling for the three huge doors, all of which stood open. Hysterical, drug-sodden, mad with fear, they battled their way.

Fryer was lying motionless; he had cracked his head on a table and been knocked unconscious.

Marion looked at Hammond, wondering what his reaction was behind his expressionless mask. She saw that the Department Z men were forcing some kind of order; lifting the fallen, supporting the injured, marshalling the chaotic stream of near-maniacs.

Hammond leaned forward.

'They'll run into the police,' he said. 'So will Fryer's tommy-gun gents. We'll have had full value when it's over.'

The faint haze which had filled the room began to clear.

Of the crowd, no more than a dozen had kept their places; all of them wore gas-masks, and all, Marion imagined, were the decent-looking couples who had been so noticeably out of place.

Hammond pushed his chair back and stood up.

'That's the end of the performance, I think,' he said. 'We'll be able to take our masks off in a few minutes.' As he spoke, the last of the crowd disappeared, and the Errols, with the rest of the Department Z men, sauntered towards the middle of the room.

'Good show,' Mike Errol said, his voice distorted by his mask. 'Value for money, eh, Bruce?'

Then he looked reproachfully towards Marion, who had started to laugh.


It was a little before midnight.

The revelry at the Lamplighter had been over for nearly two hours. The few people who had been there for genuine enjoyment had been released, most of them more than willing to admit that whatever measures had been taken to clean up the Lamplighter were justified. The police were in possession of the place, while Hammond had asked Superintendent Miller how it had been possible for the club to be as blatant a dope-house as London could have had for years.

Miller, a large, dusty-looking man, who fitted his name to perfection, was in Hammond's flat, where Marion, the Errols and a few others of the Department's men had gathered together. Fryer was in the spare room, where Hilary had been. He had regained consciousness, but was tied to the bed; Hammond had considered it wise to keep him in some uncertainty as to his immediate fate.

Miller brushed back his moustache as Hammond put the question about the police failure to close up the Lampllghter.

'It's only been open ten days,' he said. 'We've heard fairly disquieting rumours, and were planning a raid. Can't say any more than that, Mr. Hammond.' He spoke in the severe, but restrained, tones of one who considered the matter to be none of Hammond's business.

'All right, no recriminations! Your men will probably sweep up more than a dusting of cocaine off the floor—and what about the tommy-gun merchants?'

'There were eight of them,' Miller said, and smiled appreciatively. 'The tear-gas was quite an idea.'

'English?' Hammond asked.

Miller scowled. 'Excepting a couple of Irishmen, yes. What I want to know is, where did they get the guns?'

'That's an interesting point,' said Hammond slowly, 'but I'll risk one guess. The Home Guard command, where this trouble first started, has probably had its stores raided. I wish ——' he paused. 'Well, that doesn't matter. We'll check if any equipment is missing from Dorset.' He was looking at Miller yet hardly seeing him, and Miller appeared to understand that he was thinking further ahead than the events of the Lamplighter.

The Superintendent stood up.

'I'll be getting along,' he said. 'If there's anything else you want, let me know. I'll be at the Yard most of the night I fancy,' he added lugubriously. 'There never is much sleep when you fellows get around.'

He nodded in a resigned way as he went out.

Marion watched Hammond, but did not speak. She felt the eyes of the Errols turned towards her, and saw that Mike held a finger to his lips, exhorting silence.

She was amazed at the thoroughness with which the raid on the Lamplighter had been carried out. She realised that Hammond had had one thing in mind all along, and everything and everyone must be bent to that purpose. It was a little frightening, particularly from a man who appeared lazy, good humoured, and just a little too handsome to be anything but a play-boy.

Now, he beamed on all of them. 'There's good children,' he said. 'Not a squeak out of any of you. Has anyone any ideas?'

Mike crossed his legs.

'If you haven't thought enough for the lot of us,' he began, 'you—'

'Ought to be summoned for false pretences,' completed Mark spiritedly.

'Who wants ideas, anyhow?' demanded Davidson. He was the tall, calm man Marion had seen following Loftus from the flat earlier in the day. Carruthers she already knew comparatively well. He was wider awake than Davidson, and was smoothing down his fair hair while leaning as far back in an easy chair as the chair permitted.

'I'll tell you what,' said Mike slowly.

'Yes?' asked Mark.

'If we had some beer—'

Wally Davidson sat upright abruptly.

'What's that?' he asked.

'Mark said what about you going to get some beer?' said Carruthers mildly.

'Oh!' Davidson spoke disgustedly. 'Why can't he speak clearly? I thought he said would I have some.' He settled back in the chair, while Hammond levered himself up from the arms of his, and went towards his cocktail cabinet.

'I got some in,' he said. 'Drink away, chaps. I'm going to see Fryer.'

Mike said quickly: 'Do you want—'

'Any help?' completed Mark.

'From anyone?' added Carruthers.

'Not yet,' said Hammond. 'Not yet, just get yourselves drunk.'

He pushed open the bedroom door, then closed it behind him.

'Fryer, I made Esteven talk without much trouble, but I expect to have more bother from you. I may as well tell you from the start, it won't be any good, because I intend to get from you what I want.'

Fryer said nothing; there was venom in his dark eyes. Hammond's voice went on, almost expressionlessly, except that it held a deadly note. 'Don't kid yourself with the belief that it can't happen here, Fryer. You see, I've spent a lot of time in France recently. I was in France when the Huns came. I saw a lot of things that I won't forget, no matter how long I live. And,' went on Hammond, very slowly, 'I told myself that whenever the chance came to pay a little back, in kind, I'd take it. You're supposed to be an American, Fryer, but you're a Hun, and you're a Nazi. It doesn't matter what I do to you, I can't pay back more than a fraction of what the French owe the Huns.'

He stopped, and Fryer muttered: 'You wouldn't dare! You're in England—'

Hammond said: 'On the contrary, I would.'

Then, very slowly, he went to the door and turned the key in the lock.

## 18
## MEANS OF PERSUASION

Marion heard the key turn in the lock. So did the others, as they draped themselves about the settee and armchairs, each holding a glass of beer.

Little sound came from the other room.

The conversation in the lounge was desultory. Marion imagined that the four men knew what Hammond was doing; she had a fair idea herself. She had seen him make Esteven talk, and she believed that Fryer would be a more difficult subject.

She thought of all he had told her, and all that she had learned from other sources. She knew the vital importance of finding an early solution to the problem; she knew the importance of finding out before the twenty-first of April four days hence.

Then abruptly the door opened.

Hammond came through, in his shirt-sleeves. His face was very pale, and before speaking he went to the cabinet and helped himself to a strong whisky. He drank it slowly, and some of his colour returned. Finishing the drink, he lit a cigarette.

'We're making progress,' he said, 'good progress. One of the answers is in the Home Guard. I thought it was. Fryer's managed to get a squad of men in the section down there who'll do what he wants—actually they always worked for him, and for Berlin.' Hammond was speaking swiftly. 'He's named them; I don't think there'll be any more trouble that end.'

Mike Errol said: 'Good work, Bruce. Anything else?'

'Cavendish's place was fired to try to make sure that the meeting takes place at Crayshaw's home, that's also ascertained. Another thing—' he smiled a little. 'Bill will be sending in a good report soon, I think.'

Mark snapped: 'What do you mean?' The others leaned forward quickly and Marion was affected by the sudden tension. 'The body with his papers was planted, because they wanted us to think Craigie was dead. They've got him, and they want to squeeze information out of him.' His smile seemed to freeze on his lips, then. 'Fryer doesn't know where he is.'

Mark snapped: 'The swine may be lying—'

Hammond looked at him oddly.

'No. Fryer won't lie any more just now,' he said, and left that subject abruptly. 'There's someone else in this, but Fryer doesn't know who. We'll find out, please God, before they start on Craigie. Because if they start on Craigie, they won't use amateurs in the art of persuasion.' He paused, and the silence was absolute. Then he went on: 'I'll get things going with the H.G. people, and get that squad under arrest. Fryer seems to think they were relying on the squad for the big job on the twenty-first. He doesn't know what the big job is,' he added. 'He only knows what I know. It's either to do with the manoeuvres or the conference. We've got four days to find out.'

To Marion Caroll, the next two days were bewildering, and she did little that appeared to contribute anything towards the problem.

She saw Hammond only occasionally.

He went down to Weymouth, she knew, and six men were put under close arrest. He called on Hilary Crayshaw who was in a nursing-home near Piccadilly, each time with Marion. The girl was no longer delirious, although it was obvious that she was ill. She stuck to her story that she had lost the cross which her father had given her. She knew of no reason why she should have been attacked.

Once Marion had seen Loftus. He had been able to satisfy himself that the dead body was not that of Gordon Craigie, but unable to identify either of the dead men. All the servants and members of the Cavendish family who had been at the Hall were accounted for.

Cavendish himself had been in London.

Loftus, Marion knew, was in Craigie's office, trying to co-ordinate the information which reached him from all manner of places. Marion gained a glimpse, a small glimpse, into the wide-spread activities of the Department. She learned a little more when Lois and Christine spent a flying visit to London, and they lunched together at Hammond's flat which, for the time being at least, was more Marion's than his.

Marion wished she had something more definite to do.

She was relieved that Emile was improving, touched that he frequently demanded to see her, and yet worried lest any further attack should be made on him. None, so far, had been attempted, and no further effort had been made to get at Hilary Crayshaw.

It was about mid-day on the nineteenth of April that the telephone rang. Marion raised the receiver, and heard Hershall's voice say abruptly: 'Give me Hammond, please.'

Hearing Hammond entering the flat at the moment, Marion covered the mouthpiece and called out urgently: 'It's the Prime Minister!'

'Thanks.' He took the receiver. 'Hammond speaking, sir.'

'Well?' asked Hershall without wasting time.

'There's nothing more definite to report,' said Hammond.

'Hm.' A pause. 'What do you want me to do?'

'Go ahead as arranged, please.'

'At Crayshaw's?'

'Definitely.' Hammond spoke without hesitation. 'No purpose can be served by altering arrangements at this stage. If anything transpires at the last minute there can be a cancellation, I suppose?'

'I don't want to leave anything to the last minute,' said Hershall. Then more slowly: 'Hammond, you're not making any mistake, are you?'

'Has Crayshaw been protesting?' asked Hammond, and Marion watched the way his jaw tightened.

'I'm told that he's been followed, that he's watched wherever he goes,' said Hershall. 'I haven't seen him myself, Hammond, but—' the Prime Minister paused.

Hammond said slowly: 'I think it would be a good idea, sir, if you told him that the police have reason to believe that his life is in danger, and that he's being protected. That should cover all reasonable queries, and help us to work.'

'I see,' said Hershall crisply. He paused. 'I wish I had more time to discuss it—'

'I don't think it will be long now, sir.'

'I hope not,' said Hershall. 'I certainly hope not.'

He rang off, and Hammond replaced the receiver, smiling a little. He turned to Marion. 'Crayshaw's getting worried, darling, he's worried enough to put in a plaintive protest—though not in person—to the Prime Minister.'

'Why are you so sure it's Crayshaw?' asked Marion.

'Sure?' He shrugged. 'I don't quite know why, I don't even know that I am, but everything points towards it. He could be implicated indirectly, but I don't think so. Of course—' He paused, and Marion said a moment later:

'Bruce, you're the most irritating man in the world!'

'Marion,' said Hammond easily, 'was that merely a sweeping generalisation, or a personal complaint?'

'Oh, very definitely a personal complaint. You were on the point of telling me what you really think. You never have reached farther than that.'

Hammond smiled. 'That's true enough. I nearly told you then, and thought better of it. I haven't told the others, because I can't offer anything in the way of proof. I would tell you, but I think the knowledge might be dangerous. Have you prepared anything for lunch?'

'Not yet. I was going to—'

'Don't dare suggest a snack,' said Hammond. 'We'll try the Regal. I'm hungry, and you'll pine away if you go on having cups of tea because there's no one here to enjoy a square meal with you. Hat and coat, powder and paint. Away with you—damn!'

He broke off at the ringing of the telephone. Marion, already halfway to the bedroom, paused as he answered it. Eager at the thought of lunching with him, she had stopped asking herself why her heart always leapt when he entered the room. So far she had not admitted to herself that she was in love.

He was a dangerous man to love; and in any case there was little likelihood that he would feel that way about her. She had never known a man so utterly possessed by his work.

She expected the telephone to bring word that he was wanted elsewhere, and was prepared to meet an expression of real, or assumed, regret. Instead, he put down the receiver with a grin of boyish triumph, and danced across the room, seizing her round the waist.

'What is it?' she demanded urgently. 'Don't be a beast, Bruce, what is it?'

'Invitation to a waltz,' said Hammond. 'In other words a luncheon party for three. You're coming with me, my sweet, to Sir Noel Crayshaw's Audeley Street house. There is a matter he wants to discuss.'

Hammond was thinking of the first time he had entered Crayshaw's house, when he had carried Hilary over the threshold, and then heard a story he had wanted to disbelieve, but which everyone assured him was true—even Hilary herself. He recognised the aged servant who opened the front door and then led the way to a large room on the left.

Crayshaw was standing in front of the vast fireplace. Hammond eyed the well-knit figure, the dark, rather old-fashioned clothes, the deep blue eyes, with something akin to respect. There was power in Crayshaw; Hershall had it, he knew other men, though not many, who emanated the same kind of aura.

Crayshaw's greying beard and moustache made him look like a Frenchman of the early 1900's; in his gesture as he welcomed them there was also a Gallic touch.

'How do you do, Miss Caroll—and you, Mr. Hammond? And what will you drink?'

'Sherry, please,' said Marion.

'If there is a whisky and soda, thanks,' said Hammond.

'Miss Caroll is wise, I think. Sherry is the only drink that does not affect good food.' He smiled, as he handed Hammond the whisky. 'Mr. Hammond, your concern for me is—shall we say?—a kindly thought, but I wanted to see you in the hope that I could persuade you that it is unnecessary.'

Hammond smiled in return. 'You can't be too sure of that, can you?'

'Reasonably so,' murmured Crayshaw.

'Each man has his own interpretation of what is reasonable,' said Hammond easily. 'I must remind you that your view that your daughter's hanging was self-inflicted was contrary to mine. There is ample evidence now that you were wrong.'

'Indeed?' Crayshaw's manner suggested a mild interest but no real concern for what had happened to Hilary.

'There have also been other attacks on her life.'

'I was not advised of them,' said Crayshaw sharply.

'We hoped it wouldn't be necessary to worry you,' Hammond said. 'The attacks were frustrated, and she is now in a place where she will be safe from any further attempts. But you will readily see, sir, the possibility that if she is in danger, you are also.'

'I hardly see why,' said Crayshaw.

'We—ell,' said Hammond, 'I have to take some decisions on my own. This is one. By the way, how did you know that my men were watching you?'

Crayshaw said suavely: 'I was recently advised that the police had taken this interest in me, and I wondered why. Immediately I knew the theory on which they were working, I wondered if you could be in any way implicated. And a few inquiries—' Crayshaw smiled, 'elicited the obvious result. So I asked you to lunch, the better to discuss the matter.

Aren't you convinced, Mr. Hammond, that I can take care of myself?'

'No,' said Bruce bluntly.

'You are very downright,' murmured Crayshaw.

'There isn't much point in beating about the bush,' said Hammond, smiling amiably. 'I have to be careful, Crayshaw; I can't take too many chances. Today, for instance, I was followed by two men, just in case an attack should be made on me while coming here, or going away.'

Crayshaw said: 'You appear to have an attack-fixation.'

Hammond chuckled. 'They say that experience makes fools wise.'

On his words the door opened and the old servant announced lunch. Marion was aware that Crayshaw appeared to have anticipated the man's coming. It was uncanny, she thought; and then she told herself that she was being a fool, that Crayshaw had given instructions for luncheon to be served at a precise moment. He was not likely to allow unpunctuality, even to a matter of seconds.

They went into a large dining room, the long table set at one end only. The rest of the room was dark and shadowy, the windows covered with anti-splinter net, the furniture old enough to have seen a dozen generations of men live and die. This strange combination lent an air of unnaturalness to the room and to Crayshaw.

The food was good and the conversation during the meal light and unimportant; yet all the time Marion felt that there was an unseen presence. She knew the two men were fencing for an opening, that Crayshaw was a little perturbed, for Hammond's defence was so quick and his answers unflagging.

Coffee was to be served in the other room, and Marion rose with relief at the prospect of leaving the shadows and the gloom behind them, yet the tension stayed.

Marion knew one thing; these men were enemies, and each of them was aware of it.

Crayshaw lit a cigar, leaning comfortably back in an easy chair. 'Now, Mr. Hammond, we can really try to discuss the matter and reach a mutually satisfactory result. It is a fact, you know, that I do indeed realise the possibility of danger to myself, and am therefore always accompanied, although not ostentatiously, by a man who can take care of any emergency.'

Hammond smiled: 'Point to me, you know. The danger is admitted.'

Crayshaw spoke a little sharply.

'Any man in my position is always in some danger, particularly in these days, when a share in the nation's war effort is important, and enemies of the state abound.'

'It is precisely because of that,' murmured Bruce, 'that I want to make sure that your bodyguard doesn't go wrong, sir.'

'Surely I should be the Judge of what is necessary?' said Crayshaw, and Hammond's eyes narrowed as he smiled.

'We can't always be sure of what's good for us,' he murmured.

Crayshaw withdrew his cigar, staring at the tip speculatively: 'Mr. Hammond, you may be justified in what you are doing, but at least I am entitled to know why you are doing it. To say the least, I find these constant attentions irritating.'

'I'm sorry about that,' said Hammond. The tone in which he uttered the words was clearly calculated to annoy the millionaire, and what little of Crayshaw's cheeks were visible above his beard, coloured.

'I don't like your manner, Hammond.'

'We—ell,' said Hammond, 'that's understandable. But supposing we really get down to business Crayshaw? You know as well as I do that I don't trust you. I don't trust a lot of people, although that's no proof that I'm right; but while I have my particular job to do, I'll go on doing it as I think best. Of course, I could change my mind—' he paused.

'Explain yourself,' snapped Crayshaw.

'If you would tell me just why you are so anxious to make sure that your Dorset house is used for the coming conference, and just why a Dr. Brice was frequently in attendance on you there, if you would tell me why you really employed Ferdinand to watch your daughter—well, with a satisfactory explanation of those things, I might withdraw. I'd like to withdraw,' Hammond added earnestly. 'Only you are stopping me, you know.'

He stopped; and Marion felt her heart racing. This was a challenge, tantamount to a direct accusation.

# 19

## 'SNATCH'

C rayshaw's body appeared to have shrunk. He leaned well back in his chair, his right hand drumming a ceaseless tattoo on the arm. The *tick-tock-tick-tock* of a clock in one corner of the room reminded Marion of the interval signal of the B.B.C. before a speech from some significant broadcaster.

Crayshaw spoke at last. 'My dear fellow, you are paid—if you will forgive me mentioning it—to suspect the whole world. But suspicion is one thing, mania another. I must warn you that, however sympathetic I may be towards this remarkable example of your rather excessive zeal, the consequence of further annoyance will be serious.'

'Oh, come,' said Hammond. 'I don't let go that easily.'

Crayshaw's eyes glittered. He paced the room in front of the fireplace, then paused and shrugged. 'I am willing to humour you to a certain extent, but don't go too far, Hammond. Well then, it is true that I should like my house to be used, but I have done nothing to try to ensure that. I have been attended by a young doctor in Dorset because my regular medical adviser there has been called up. I employed Ferdinand as a mentor for my daughter, on the advice of her doctor. You appear to have affixed some highly coloured explanation to facts which are simple and quite lacking in mystery. Where is my daughter?'

'Where you won't get her,' Hammond assured him. He stood up abruptly, waiting for Marion as Crayshaw approached him, hands clenched by his sides. Hammond pressed the bell at the fireplace, and was at the door when the servant came.

'Our coats, please,' he said brusquely.

Crayshaw said nothing, but continued to stare at them his eyes glittering, as they prepared to go. The servant opened the door, and they stepped on to the porch.

'Hurry,' Hammond said, and gripped Marion's arm.

She was alerted by his manner, by the sudden haste of his movements. He glanced swiftly up and down, seeing a Bentley at one end of the street and the Errols beside it. He half-ran towards them, still gripping Marion's arm.

It was when they were barely half-way, that another car turned into the street, travelling at considerable speed. Hammond stopped running and his voice was sharp and peremptory: 'Get down, quickly.'

The car passed them, but nothing appeared to happen. Marion raised her head and looked behind her: she saw something fly from the window of the car to Crayshaw's house.

Hammond said hoarsely: 'Keep down!'

The explosion came on his words, fierce and deafening, making her ears ring, flinging her against the wall under which they were crouching. She felt the jar as she hit the rough surface, then felt Hammond move by her side. He had leapt up, and was running back towards Crayshaw's house.

The front of it was blown in; the windows gaped, and through them he could see the wreckage of the room where, with Marion, he had been sitting less than five minutes before. He climbed over the debris, heedless of the gathering crowd.

Half of the ceiling of the room was down, leaving a fringe dangling crazily. The coals had been sprayed about the room, while flames were already shooting from the seat of one of the chairs.

Hammond stepped carefully through the doorway and into the hall, meeting the old servant shaking in fright.

'Where's Sir Noel?'

'He—' muttered the old man, 'he—'

Then Hammond saw Crayshaw stepping from another room at the far end of the passage.

Hammond said slowly: 'So you're all right?'

Crayshaw opened his mouth with an odd clicking sound.

'Yes, I—what happened? James, what—'

Hammond said: 'The front room was blown to nothing. Anyone in there would have gone the same way. It's lucky I moved when I did, isn't it? And now—' he paused, 'perhaps you'll admit that you're in danger.'

He did not wait to say anything more, or to hear what Crayshaw said, but hurried down the steps again.

It took him and the Errols twenty minutes to reassure the police who were at first distrustful of their cards. A cordon had been put about the house, and already the debris was being cleared away by men summoned from a nearby demolition squad.

'Well, anyway,' said Mike Errol, 'the bus is all right, so I can give you a lift somewhere.'

'Ye—es,' said Hammond. 'The flat, I think, but—' he paused. 'Who's watching the back of the house?'

'Wally Davidson and Carruthers,' said Mike promptly.

'They ought to be all right,' Hammond deliberated, turning some coins over in his pocket. 'Yes, they should be all right,

THE DAY OF DISASTER

but I wouldn't like to swear to it. You'd better back them up,' he added at last. 'Keep an eye on Crayshaw wherever he goes, and remember you're expecting a snatch.'

To the Errols the word apparently had some meaning. To Marion it was Greek. She turned it over in her mind until they had pulled up outside the Jermyn Street house in a taxi.

'An abbreviation, I suppose?' she asked.

Hammond smiled. 'Certainly an abbreviation, being shorter than kidnapping and less reminiscent of the Lyceum.'

He helped her out, paid the cabby and then went upstairs with a hand on her arm.

Once in the flat, he turned urgently towards her: 'Are you all right?' His voice was gruff.

'Yes, of course.'

'You're sure? You——' He released her suddenly, with a short laugh. 'Yes, of course you are. I'm going crazy. You've scratched your chin.' He did not refer to the urgency in his voice, or explain the expression in his eyes when he had asked whether she was all right; but she believed she knew the answer, and her heart was singing as she went into the bathroom, finding that a piece of debris had cut her just beneath the chin. Hammond entered the room and dabbed at it with cotton wool. He insisted on dressing it, saying as he did so: 'Yes, I expect a snatch, I think they'll try to handle it that way.' He smiled bleakly. 'It would be clever, but then the whole plot's damnably clever.'

'Bruce,' said Marion quietly, 'stop dabbing at my chin and tell me what you mean. Stop talking in riddles and acting as if you had second sight.'

'Second sight?' he repeated. 'Nonsense, my sweet, first was good enough. I made it clear to Crayshaw that I didn't trust him, so clear that he knew he had to act quickly. He had a pre-arranged plan; I should have known that was likely. I think,' he added musingly, 'that I did. Put your head over a bit, I can't see what I'm doing with this plaster.'

'I don't want—'

'Hush, don't interrupt! I might be on the verge of some amazing revelations, you never know.' He finished putting on the sticking-plaster, and then said: 'It was simple. A car was waiting at the back of the house. Crayshaw leaned against the mantel-shelf and at the same time pressed the button of the service bell. I knew something was coming then, and decided that we should beat it.'

'For heaven's sake, fill in the gaps!' pleaded Marion.

'But that's just what I'm doing,' said Hammond in genuine surprise. 'Crayshaw had the car waiting, with the H.E. stuff. The press on the bell told the old servant to pass a message to the driver of the car, which was driven off at once. Crayshaw would have slipped out of the room, as he did—I found him in a back room when I returned—and you and I would have been adorning the railings in pieces. Not nice, is it?'

Marion sat down abruptly.

'No,' she said.

'Of course,' mused Hammond, 'it was very clever indeed. You and I would be off the writing-list, and the whole show would have seemed like an attempt on his life. He must have thought of that well ahead of me, but I think I encouraged him to believe I've assumed he's in danger, don't you?'

Marion said: 'Ye—es. But you virtually told him he was a rogue.'

'I let him know that I thought he was up to funny business, but that someone else was after him. Involved, perhaps,' he added, 'but I think he got it. The attack on us, of course, he had already planned; he wanted to appear the lucky man to escape assassination. Now he'll let himself be kidnapped. I want the boys to stop him once, and then he can go.'

Marion raised her hands.

'Are you sane?'

'Good Lord, no!' exclaimed Hammond. 'Did you ever think I was? Any nurse worthy of the name should have seen the symptoms by now.' He paused, then went on: 'Seriously, I think Crayshaw knows that his one way of escape and success is to disappear as if involuntarily. I want him stopped once, so that he'll be really nervous about the Department. I've wanted him nervous, I've worked at his nerves for three days with just that one object in mind.'

'It's beginning to make sense,' said Marion.

'That's something.' His smile was boyish. 'Well, what's the next question?'

'If you're going to let him get himself kidnapped,' said Marion, 'how is it going to help?'

'Oh, that's easy,' said Hammond. 'We'll be watching and he'll be followed. You see, Marion, if I hadn't played on his nerves, if I hadn't made him realise he was being closely watched, he could have slipped away somewhere in the country and directed operations from wherever he chose, by telephone, personal contact, half a dozen different ways. Now I've forced him to go somewhere where he can't be easily traced. Accent on "easily". The obvious place for him to go is—' he paused, 'the hideout or what-have-you from which the operations have been directed right through. The place, I hope, where Craigie is being kept.'

Marion said: 'Then everything depends on you following him successfully?'

'Everything,' agreed Hammond slowly.

Marion looked at him evenly. 'What do you think is behind it, Bruce?'

Hammond hesitated. She felt a tremor of excitement at the very thought that he was going to tell her. He began to speak slowly: 'I think the conference is the first essential factor, and the manoeuvres the other. I think that—'

A sharp knock on the door interrupted him. 'Go on,' Marion urged. 'Don't answer for a moment. Bruce, please—'

She broke off as another knock sounded, louder than the first. Hammond shrugged. 'That perisher outside is in a hurry, isn't he?' He stepped to the door, opening it, standing back and smiling. 'Hallo, old chap, what brings you?'

Marion saw Loftus entering.

She had wished him to perdition a moment before. Now the half-smile he sent towards her brought an answering one from her. She watched him walk laboriously across the room with the help of his stick, and sink with relief into an easy chair. She wondered whether he would want her to hear what he had to say, but it did not, apparently, cross his mind that she should go.

'What's the trouble with Crayshaw?' he asked as soon as he was settled.

Hammond smiled. 'Trouble *via* the Prime Minister?'

'Well,' said Loftus, 'trouble isn't exactly the word, but he wants to know whether I'm quite sure that you know what you're doing. He said he was quite aware that there are some things best kept to oneself, but in the circumstances he felt that some degree of confidence might be reposed in him.' Loftus smiled crookedly. 'As sarcasm it wasn't even gentle, but it made itself felt.'

'The upshot?' asked Hammond quickly.

'He wants a full report by mid-day tomorrow. He's going to Dorset in the late afternoon and I've promised him he shall have the report on time.' Hammond looked relieved.

'Good man,' he said. 'He's given us the extra time we need, Bill, just those few hours.'

Loftus looked at him squarely. 'Why don't you loosen up?' he asked.

'It hasn't worked itself out thoroughly yet,' said Hammond, 'but it's coming. Bill, I think with a little luck and a lot of effort we could prove a case against Crayshaw. I think we could get the connecting link between him, Fryer, Esteven and the other bunch clear enough to detain him. If I were to tell the P.M. what it is, he would have to have Crayshaw detained for questioning. He positively couldn't let a man in that position go free if he knew what we know.'

'Go easy,' said Loftus. 'We're not as sure as all that yet.'

Hammond raised an eyebrow. 'You're not? Bill, the tommy-guns lifted from the Home Guard were passed through Crayshaw's place; the Dr. Brice whose record proves he was constantly in touch with spies frequently met Crayshaw and others at Crayshaw's house. Both these things are interesting factors, though not damning ones. But I'll guarantee one thing. If we put Crayshaw and his daughter face to face for an hour, we would get information that would make Crayshaw's detention imperative.'

Loftus said: 'I'll have to take your word for it.'

'You can,' said Hammond. 'But Bill, I may be wrong. I could pass on what I think to you, and you would probably act on it. If I'm wrong and you act on what I say, you're going to get a hell of a packet. I'd rather keep the kicks for myself, if there are any coming. But we're talking round the subject,' he added more sharply.

'Yes,' said Loftus dryly. 'Why not have Crayshaw hauled in, if you're as sure as that?'

'Precisely the point,' said Hammond. 'I don't want him taken yet, I want the whole show to break, I want—'

He stopped abruptly, interrupted by the shrill ringing of the telephone.

Marion, who had believed that he was getting to the point where he would tell Loftus as well as herself what was in his mind, confounded this second interruption as she had confounded the first.

Hammond answered the 'phone, and she saw him stiffen.

'Yes?' he said. 'Yes, he's here too ... you're sure ... good man, Mike, good man!' He replaced the receiver, and swung round, his eyes shining. 'Another step forward,' he went on, his voice on a high key. 'Crayshaw just left the house on foot, and an attempt was made to kidnap him in Piccadilly—my God, he's getting desperate!'

Loftus said dazedly: 'Kidnap him!'

Hammond gave a brief résumé of his conclusions, then went on: 'The Errols baulked it, Crayshaw was full of thanks and gratitude, then took a taxi to his City office. The Errols are there, with Davidson and Carruthers. Bill, get to that 'phone, send at least another six of the boys there. We mustn't let him slip away without being followed.'

Loftus drew a deep breath.

'You're more temperamental than a musical comedy star,' he said. 'Heaven help the woman who marries you!' He winked at Marion, as he got busy on the telephone. Marion saw that something of Hammond's excitement had transferred itself to the other man. After the instructions had gone out, Hammond told Loftus in brief what he had told Marion, talking quickly, almost agitatedly. When he had finished there was a short silence in the room.

Marion broke it.

'Bruce, if he's going to disappear, isn't it obvious that he'll go in the black-out?'

Hammond chuckled.

'Obvious that he'll try, no more. I'm going to be the most disappointed man in England if he does get away without any trace.' He was suddenly anxious. 'The other fellows can make sure of him, Bill, can't they?'

'If anyone can, yes,' said Loftus. 'I'm not going to start worrying myself in case Crayshaw slips through our fingers when we've nearly a dozen men watching him.'

'But he can adopt some kind of disguise,' insisted Marion, 'and you needn't say that's Lyceum-ish, Bruce, it could be done well enough to make him look different at a casual glance, or a glance in the dark. Supposing he shaved off his beard and moustache, for instance?'

Hammond said: 'You're beginning to make me feel uncomfortable. His beard and moustache, yes... I'd assumed that he had to keep those, but—'

For the third time he was interrupted. He went to the telephone and lifted it quickly, grew more eager as he listened, and then snapped: 'Yes ... a black Rolls-Royce ... eh? ... that was his car, all right, what did they take him away in? ... an Austin 20 with a spray of fresh white paint on the offside rear wing ...' His voice was rising as he spoke; Loftus had got to his feet and was standing near him, in the grip of an excitement emanating from Hammond's tense voice. 'Two bunches of you after it? ... yes, I'll get it put out at once.'

He banged the receiver down, and snapped: 'He was snatched as he walked out of the building to his car, and bundled into a black Austin, but you'll have gathered that. The Errols are in their Bentley after him. Davidson and Carruthers are also on the road. We want a general police call out to have that car traced but not apprehended. We must find where he goes.'

'We'll find out,' said Loftus grimly.

He contacted with Miller, who put out the call. Reports were telephoned from various points along the road to Scotland Yard, and relayed to Loftus and Hammond at the flat.

Staines, Egham, Camberley, Hook, Basingstoke, then on the Salisbury Road, through Whitchurch and Andover, south-wards to Amesbury, Salisbury itself, Shaftesbury.

Hammond said: 'His place is near Dorchester. It looks as if he's going there.'

'Ye—es,' said Loftus. 'It's getting dark, but he'll make it before the black-out.' His hair was dishevelled, as was Hammond's, and he was sitting over the telephone, ready to lift the receiver at the first quiver of the bell.

The telephone bell rang.

'My turn, I think,' said Hammond. 'This should be from the nearest town to his home ... hallo, yes, speaking ... *what?*'

He shouted the word.

He asked for something to be repeated, speaking in a tense but otherwise unfamiliar voice, grunted, replaced the receiver, and then turned to face them.

'The car's reached his place,' he told the others harshly. 'But Crayshaw's body had been thrown out. Yes, quite dead.'

20

# CRAYSHAW GRANGE

While Loftus and Marion were staring at Hammond and trying to realise the full import of what he said, Hammond moved to his chair, picked up a note book, and began to read the quick jottings he had made. There were notes of the towns through which the car had gone, and of messages telephoned from the Errols and from the Davidson-Carruthers car. Before either of the others spoke, he said sharply: 'It doesn't necessarily finish there. The car was twice out of sight for twenty minutes or more.'

'Well, what difference does that make?' demanded Loftus.

'They tried to make us believe that one dead man was Craigie,' said Hammond. 'They might be trying to make us believe that this dead man is Crayshaw.' He thrust his hands deep in his pockets, rose a little on his toes, and then said: 'Has Hershall got an understudy?'

Loftus frowned. 'There's a man named Fenn in the Foreign Office, similar enough to him to get cheered in Whitehall sometimes. What's the idea?'

'Will he take a chance?'

'Probably, if he knows what it is.'

'Right!'

Marion had imagined that the effect of the latest report would be to depress him thoroughly. Instead he looked eager and alert. 'Now listen, both of you. I think that the plan for the twenty-first is neither more nor less than the kidnapping of the Prime Minister.'

He could not have caused a bigger sensation had he thrown a bomb in the room.

Both Loftus and Marion stared at him as if he had gone mad.

Hammond said sharply: 'Surely you can see what a coup it would be? If the Nazis could get Hershall, bang would go the greater part of the British war effort. What a triumph for them!'

'Snatching—the P.M.,' said Loftus weakly.

'Now come, grow up,' said Hammond, but he was smiling. 'You see why I kept it to myself. You see what you two would have said had I advanced the suggestion twenty-four hours ago?'

'If you'll give just two reasons why—' began Loftus, to be cut short as Hammond said:

'No, Bill, I can't give reasons off-hand; they need explaining and there isn't time. Can you get that Foreign Office cover here in the next hour?'

Loftus hesitated, and then said: 'I'd better go to see him.' He pulled himself from his chair, stepped to the telephone and dialled a number. He was connected quickly. A brief conversation ensued, and then he rang off. 'He's still there,' he told Hammond. 'I'll ring you if anything further turns up. What about the P.M.?'

'I'm going to ring him,' said Hammond reflectively. 'I wonder how he'll take it? I wonder—'

He dialled the Prime Minister's number, glancing at his watch as he did so.

'He's probably having a nap,' Loftus called from the door. 'He does, about this time. May his temper be sweet.'

'Go away,' said Hammond testily.

A secretary answered him; he was referred to a second, and then to a third. To them all he gave his name and insisted that he must speak to Hershall in person, and on an urgent matter. After some delay he heard Hershall's voice, sharp, forbidding.

'All right, what is it?'

'I think we're ready for something to break,' said Hammond briskly. 'Crayshaw, or a man purporting to be Crayshaw, has been killed near Crayshaw Grange, sir.'

He heard an exclamation, and then Hershall's voice reached him again, the powerful voice of a man in control.

'You're sure of this?'

'Either it's Crayshaw or someone very like him,' said Hammond. 'And I think it means we've forced them into acting quicker than they planned. I want—' he paused, then amended: 'I wonder if you have any objection to it being said that you're going to Crayshaw Grange tonight, instead of tomorrow.'

'What the dickens are you talking about?' demanded Hershall.

'Loftus tells me there is a man who can be passed off as you, sir,' said Hammond doggedly. 'I would like to use him, in Dorset. If you could telephone the Grange and say you will be along before midnight, it would be a great help.'

After a pause, Hershall said:

'What exactly are you driving at, Hammond?'

Marion saw Hammond's lips tighten. He appeared to be marshalling his thoughts before he spoke, but Hershall did not hurry him.

'From the time that I first heard that you were likely to be at the Grange, sir,' said Hammond, 'I tried to find a motive for what has happened. It could hardly be concerned directly with manoeuvres, but the manoeuvres obviously played a part in it, since we had the H.G. involved. The conference was important, but after all, the information there could be obtained in bits and pieces, and the preparations, the warnings, everything that has happened suggests something rather larger than a spy at the conference. If that was all we would hardly have been warned.'

Hershall said tersely: 'Go on.'

'In fact, the warnings seemed to be deliberately aimed at postponing the conference. You'll recall that we got the warnings only after the letter from Langham, in France, had been found. The plans were seriously disturbed by that, and so an attempt was made to confuse the issue and to get the date altered. That didn't matter, because a new date would be fixed, and they could learn that as easily as they learned of this one. Anyhow, sir, it seemed to me that the conference as such wasn't the important thing, but that its being staged at Crayshaw Grange was.'

Marion saw the way Hammond's free left hand was clenching and unclenching; clearly he was nervous, although nothing of that was reflected in his voice.

'The Grange is near the coast,' Hammond went on. 'The manoeuvres take place near the coast and include plans for a mock-invasion, with the Home Guard taking place. We know that fifth-columnists were with the Home Guard, and the fact that some have been eliminated doesn't mean they all have. Keeping those facts in mind, sir, I wondered how they could best be used to create an effective and really dangerous blow to the country. I thought that it would be comparatively easy for you to be kidnapped and taken out to sea. The invasion exercises to take place with actual craft, I think, would give a perfect opportunity for this. One boat amongst many, if its crew and passengers were in uniform, would hardly be noticed. Do you follow me?'

There was a long pause from the other end.

Then Hershall said: 'Hammond, I cannot believe that Sir Noel Crayshaw would be a party to any such infamy.'

'I haven't all the data available yet, sir,' said Hammond tensely, 'but I am quite sure that the attempt was to be made with Crayshaw's help—whether deliberate or unwitting I don't yet know. At all events, if they believe you are going down tonight, and we have someone to take your place, I think we can force them to act sooner than they intended to.'

There was another pause, and then Hershall said: 'All right, Hammond.'

Hammond drew in so deep a breath of relief that it could be heard throughout the room. 'There's just one other thing,' he said carefully, 'if you're known to be in London all the evening—'

Hershall actually chuckled. 'Don't worry about that, I will have it put around that I've left for the country. I'll be here all night, call me as soon as you have some results, no matter what time it is.'

'I will, sir,' said Hammond warmly.

He looked at Marion as he replaced the receiver, and his eyes were very bright.

'Now all we want is word from Bill,' he said. 'Marion, we're on the last lap.'


Gordon Craigie had no idea that he was at Crayshaw Grange.

He knew that he was in an attic room; but the windows

were in the ceiling, and the glass was toughened; he had made several efforts to break it, but unsuccessfully.

The room was furnished comfortably enough, with a couple of easy chairs, a bed, a shelf of books. A small bathroom and lavatory led from it, and there was plenty of hot water. Since the first interview with Crayshaw, however, he had seen no one but the man who had brought his food. He was, in fact, expecting the man to bring his evening meal at any moment, for it was nearly half-past seven.

But it was Crayshaw who entered. He moved forward with a cat-like tread, standing eventually between Craigie and the shelf of books he had been contemplating.

'I want your full attention, Craigie,' he said.

Craigie shrugged.

'You have it.'

'Ah, very accommodating of you, Craigie. You are, perhaps, a little bored? I am about to rectify that, for tonight you will have, for a few hours, distinguished company.'

'Yes?' Craigie's voice held the slightly bored note of polite formality.

'Most distinguished company,' Crayshaw said softly. 'Indeed, the Prime Minister himself.'

Craigie crossed his legs, smiling a little.

'Don't you think your optimistic announcement may be a little premature?'

Crayshaw snapped: 'Your men had no idea what was planned!'

'We—ell,' said Craigie, 'nor did I. But a little hard reasoning made it fairly obvious that you were hoping to kidnap Hershall.' He shrugged. 'I don't think you'll succeed.'

'I'll succeed,' Crayshaw said shortly. 'He's coming tonight. The plans have been altered.' The words rose in a crescendo of triumph.

'I don't think you'll succeed, Crayshaw.' Craigie smiled again, and picked up his book.

Crayshaw knocked it out of his hands.

'Listen to me! I'm taking you and Hershall across the Channel, and once you're there the whole of the Continental radio link-up will broadcast the news. It will spread like wildfire, no one in this country will fail to know about it. Hershall and Craigie—the Prime Minister and the Secret Service leader, the two most important men in England today.'

Craigie said: 'Don't be absurd, I don't rate in the first hundred. And Crayshaw, I'm getting hungry—'

'Hungry!' shouted Crayshaw. 'You'll know what it is to starve, to beg for bread and water, you'll know what it is to plead for mercy! You and Hershall, you'll be tortured and starved, you'll be broken in body and in spirit, you'll give all the information we want, you'll do just as you're told. Hungry! You don't know what is going to happen to you, you don't know—'

Craigie snapped: 'Stop this drivel!'

He stood up abruptly, forcing Crayshaw to step back. Crayshaw's right hand dropped to his pocket, and Craigie's eyes narrowed again, but he made no further comment. He watched the bearded man's tongue running along his lips, and then Crayshaw spoke in a more controlled voice.

'Drivel, is it? You'll learn differently, Craigie; you'll learn how serious it is. And *I* conceived this plan, Craigie. It was I who saw the possibilities, and obtained permission from Berchtesgaden. The conception and the execution has been mine from start to finish!'

Craigie said: 'Execution is a well-chosen word, Crayshaw.'

He thought the man would strike him. Crayshaw half drew his right hand from his pocket, and Craigie saw the glint of steel. 'Soon you'll regret that, Craigie, very soon.' He laughed, and the sound was not pleasant. 'Listen, Craigie, Hammond came to me this morning and told me what he thought. The darned fool, he gave himself away! So I arranged to be kidnapped, and without doubt, I was followed. So a man *looking* like me, a man with marks on the body exactly like mine, a man whose teeth have been stopped exactly like mine, was thrown out of the kidnappers' car. He was quite dead, Craigie. Do you understand now?'

Craigie said slowly: 'I've always understood.'

'You fool!' snapped Crayshaw, and slapped the Chief of Department Z across the face. 'You've no realisation of the immensity of this thing; you don't understand that you are finished, that Hershall is finished, *and that the country is beaten.* Do you hear that, beaten! beaten! beaten!'

Craigie smiled, wearily.

'An assertion that's been shrieked down the ages quite a number of times, I believe. I don't recollect that it's made much difference.'

'You self-satisfied, smug, complacent English swine!' snarled Crayshaw. 'This time we've got you, we've—'

There was a tap at the door. Still pointing his gun towards Craigie, Crayshaw called out:

'What is it?'

'A message has just come through,' said a voice which Craigie did not recognise. 'The car left Downing Street fifteen minutes ago.'

Crayshaw shouted. 'It's left, he's on the way! Now you will see, Craigie, now you will see!'


The Right Honourable Graham Hershall lay on his bed smoking, deep in thought. Presently he pressed a bell for his secretary. His orders, when they came, were sharp and to the point. A car was to be placed at the disposal of Hammond and Department Z; one of his regular chauffeurs was to be at the wheel; one of his secretaries was to travel down with Fenn. The secretary, already aware of what was proposed, accepted the orders swiftly.

'Telephone at once, Jim, to cancel all appointments for this evening. Yes, the dinner-party is off. Have a car round here by seven o'clock. I'm going out of town for the night.'

'Very good, sir.'

'I hope it is,' said Hershall.

When the man had gone Hershall began to dress, muttering occasionally to himself. He did not believe Crayshaw would play this part, he said, and he was damned if he was going to stay in London while Hammond was putting his theory to the test. There was no need for him to reveal himself immediately he reached Crayshaw Grange, but: 'If there's a mill, I'm going to be at it,' said Hershall loudly, and then chuckled to himself as he finished fastening his shoes.

## 21

## TREK TO DORSET

Marion Caroll sat back against the upholstery of the big car, and looked at the men on either side of her; Loftus on her right, Hammond on her left. Because they had chosen to sit in the tonneau together, they were crowded against one another; Hammond's arm lay across her shoulders, and occasionally his fingers brushed her cheek.

She found herself trying to put thought of Bruce and Hershall aside, to concentrate on what was coming.

She did not know all that was in Hammond's mind, and she was quite sure that Loftus did not. She remembered the brief argument at the flat, when Loftus had said bluntly that nothing would keep him out of the final showdown, and she had gained courage enough to support him, and thus in turn, get his support for her own request to join the party.

A young agent named Lester was at the wheel. Little was said in the tonneau, and the atmosphere of tension was greater than Marion had ever known it. She found the same thought running through her mind time and time again: why had Hammond wanted her to play the part she had? He had suggested that she nurse Hilary Crayshaw; but it was no more than an excuse.

She was quite sure of one thing: she was glad of the way her life had changed. She saw now, that for a year or more her vision of things and people had been jaundiced, embittered; she had been close to becoming self-centred, self-pitying. All that was gone.

The Talbot sped relentlessly on through the darkness. Then suddenly the driver pulled off the main road into the car-park of an inn.

Hammond said flatly: 'Well, here we are.'

They climbed out, Loftus slipping on the cobblestones of the inn yard, and uttering a mild curse which sounded very loud through the silence.

'I've got an idea,' said Hammond. 'Let's get on the roof and bellow out to all and sundry that we've arrived!'

'For that,' said Loftus darkly, 'I'll repay you, my son.'

As they moved on into the foyer of the inn, Marion stopped abruptly.

Hammond smiled at her.

'Yes, we're nearly all here,' he said. 'We've hired the place for the night.'

The bar, a large one, was crowded by men who for the most part were too tall for the oak beams and the low, white-washed ceiling. She recognised the Errols, Carruthers and Davidson, several of those who had been at the Lamplighter, and at least a dozen others.

The din which greeted them subsided as if by magic as Hammond spoke, his voice casual and unemphatic.

'Now chaps, you know your positions, but there are one or two other little odds and ends to keep in mind. We're half a mile from Crayshaw Grange, and we'll be within a couple of hundred yards of the house when we start in. Half a mile beyond you will see a cordon of police and Home Guard, *but*—' he paused—'the Home Guard won't be in uniform; they'll be wearing white armlets. The same applies to us, and to the police.' He took a strip of white linen from his pocket and slipped it over his wrist; Marion saw the others doing the same, and was startled at the ease and yet the thoroughness of that plan against fifth-columnists.

Loftus was handing her an armlet, and she looked up at him with a smile. Her heart was beating quickly, her cheeks were flushed with excitement.

'Nice work,' said Hammond as the rustle of movement subsided. 'The password is *"Three Blind Mice"*. Crown anyone who doesn't know it, but don't hit too hard; we'll want them for interrogation afterwards. All right?'

Twenty-odd voices replied.

'Good,' said Hammond briskly. 'Bill, the Errols and Davidson will be going straight to the house, and we'll be there in half an hour. If we're not out again in the same period, in you come, after sending word back to the police and Home Guard that you're on the move.'

He finished, drained his tankard, and grinned cheerily about him.

'Happy landings,' he said. 'And don't get hurt.'

They went out in twos and threes, smiling and cheerful, men who might be on their way to a cricket match for all their expressions indicated. Just where they were going and what was likely to happen they did not know, but Marion could imagine that had they realised it was to face a *panzer* division, they would have been as light-hearted; she was getting to know these men.

The Errols, Davidson, Hammond and Loftus alone were left with Marion in the room.

'What about me, Bruce?'

'You're coming with us, of course,' said Hammond, as if surprised. 'Unless you'd rather stay here?'

'Good Lord, no!' Marion spoke quickly, and yet she felt there was a reason which she could not understand. It did not seem part of the normal methods of Loftus and Hammond to take a woman into danger. She wished she knew the reason.

'Of course she doesn't want to stay behind,' said Loftus. 'What about another spot of beer before we go?' He turned to the bar, while Hammond and the Errols followed suit. Their tankards emptied, they waited for Hammond to move towards the door. In two cars they left the inn, and in a few minutes they had turned into the drive of Crayshaw Grange.


In the Grange, Sir Noel Crayshaw sat in an upstairs room, while in a big downstairs one a man who looked remarkably like the Prime Minister was sitting with a brandy glass in one hand and a cheroot in the other.

He was the Foreign Office man, Fenn.

He knew that the crucial test was coming soon, when for the first time he was face to face with Crayshaw. He was so like the Prime Minister that at a casual glance he would have passed muster anywhere; but at close quarters and with electric lighting, he was by no means sure that he would succeed in bluffing Crayshaw.

Loftus had given him a full resumé of the situation, and he knew the danger, but had accepted it unhesitatingly.

He had been alone for some ten minutes when the door opened and Crayshaw came in. Fenn half-rose, but Crayshaw raised a hand and approached smilingly: 'My dear Prime Minister, don't get up, don't get up!'

He shook hands, and Fenn felt the man's eyes on him, saw the gleam in them, knew that Crayshaw was filled with an unholy excitement, one which he could not altogether conceal. Fenn held his breath, half-expecting a shrieking denouncement. Then Crayshaw went back to a chair and sat down, stretching his legs luxuriously.

'I was delighted that you could come today instead of tomorrow,' he said. 'Really delighted.'

'Ah,' said Fenn, and cleared his throat. 'Come for a special reason, y'know.'

'Have you ever done anything without a motive?' asked Crayshaw, playfully wagging a finger.

'As a matter of fact, just before I left London,' said Fenn confidentially, 'I heard a rumour that you'd been found badly injured on the road. I 'phoned through, to find out, and was profoundly relieved to learn it was false.'

'Rumours, rumours,' said Crayshaw ruefully. 'Far too many of them. But they pass, my dear Prime Minister, they pass!' He leaned forward. 'But you look tired,' he added anxiously. 'D'you think you'd better have an early night?'

Fenn did indeed feel tired, although before he had sipped the brandy he had felt almost abnormally wide awake. He suspected the brandy, but knew that at all costs he must not allow his suspicions to be known.

'Early bed?' he muttered. 'Ye—es, perhaps you're right.' He yawned, while Crayshaw watched tensely the heavy-lidded eyes closing for longer and longer periods.

Then Fenn slept.

Crayshaw stood up, an eager, satisfied, anticipatory violence in every gesture. He pressed a bell, openly triumphant.

'I've got him, I've got him!'

He was at the door when it opened, and two men appeared, dressed as servants. Both were heavily built, both remarkably young for wartime civilian male employees.

'Take him up to Craigie,' Crayshaw said.

Three minutes later the door of Craigie's room was opened. Craigie put his book down and looked across at the door. He saw Crayshaw enter, then another man carrying an inert body over his shoulder.

Craigie's heart leapt.

He stood up abruptly, as Crayshaw said: 'In spite of your men, Craigie, here he is, *here he is.*'

He rubbed his hand together, while Craigie watched the newcomer being dropped into an easy chair. Craigie's face was stiff, every muscle in his body tense.

'The Prime Minister!' cried Crayshaw. 'You thought it was impossible, but I've got him, I've got him. And now I can tell you more, Craigie. This was planned in the first place to coincide with the manoeuvres, to get you and Hershall away while the manoeuvres were taking place. We changed our plans.'

Craigie was staring at Fenn, his muscles relaxing.

'You had to change them,' he said sharply.

'Never mind why! We changed them. I was always very careful to have a secondary means of escape, Craigie, and of course my interest in aeronautics and my influential position enabled me to keep a small private aeroplane here. Did you know that? I had it assembled officially as an experimental 'plane, but it will be more than experimental tonight. The sensation over the flight of Rudolf Hess will be as nothing in comparison with this—and I shall have contrived it, I shall have succeeded, no one in Berchtesgaden believed it possible.'

Craigie said: 'Crayshaw, if you—'

'Ah-ha, you are cracking!' exclaimed Crayshaw. 'You are

beginning to realise what is happening, Craigie. So, you can know more, you can—'

He stopped abruptly.

A man had entered, breathing heavily, his shoes wet from treading on the dew-covered grass outside. Crayshaw swung round towards him.

'Well, Hillier?'

The man Hillier stared at Fenn, then at Crayshaw, then back at Fenn.

'There—there's a car-load of people coming up the drive,' he muttered. 'Two cars—I think it's Hammond and the others.'

Crayshaw snapped: 'Hammond? Are you sure?'

'I think it is, Boss, I couldn't see all that well, but I think it is.'

'I'll come down,' said Crayshaw. 'Stay inside the room, and keep your gun in sight all the time. If Craigie tries anything, put him out.'

'Okay,' the man said.

Craigie watched the door close on Crayshaw, and then looked across at the unconscious man. He had recognised Fenn. His heart was racing with anticipation, it was clear that Crayshaw's scheme had been anticipated.

What he did not know was that Graham Hershall was at that moment in the grounds.

Hammond saw the door open, and with his right hand closed about a gun within his pocket, stepped into the well-lighted hall. Marion, Loftus and the Errols followed him. Davidson was to stay by the porch, in case of unexpected emergency.

They were shown into the room where Fenn had been sitting so shortly before. His unfinished cognac was at a small table by the side of an easy chair, and from his cheroot smoke was curling upwards.

Marion said *sotto voce*: 'I suppose this is the right way to go about it?'

'Not a doubt, my sweet,' said Loftus, 'not a shadow of doubt.' He, too, had his right hand in his pocket. The Errols strolled, as if aimlessly, to strategic parts of the room.

Footsteps sounded outside.

The door opened, and Crayshaw stepped through.

His expression was severe and more than a little portentous. He closed the door deliberately behind him, bowed to Marion and then said sharply:

'Well, Hammond, what is it you want now?'

Hammond smiled easily.

'You,' he said.

Crayshaw snapped: 'I have had enough of this idiocy! I had hoped that when I left London—'

Hammond interrupted quickly: 'When you were taken from London, you mean? When you allowed it to appear that you had been kidnapped and brought here? When you even went to the extent of having a dead man, disguised to look like you, thrown out of the kidnappers' car? How much longer do you think you can keep it up?'

Crayshaw stared at him for some seconds, and then very slowly smiled. The way in which his beard and moustache separated was fascinating. His red lips and white teeth were very bright against the dark hair.

'Not very much longer, my friend,' he said softly. 'There is no need to maintain it much longer. But Hammond, how glad I am that you came. I thought the body thrown out near here would be a glittering bait you couldn't resist. Loftus is with you, too. And Miss Caroll. A charming party, not to mention

JOHN CREASEY

those two earnest young men, the Errols. *All* of you, Hammond, who share suspicion of my activities.'

Hammond said: 'All except the Prime Minister.'

'My dear fellow,' said Crayshaw, 'didn't you know? A very good friend of mine, Graham Hershall. He is here now.'

Hammond stiffened.

Marion saw Loftus and the Errols stiffen also, and she realised that they wanted to make Crayshaw think that they were startled by that information. Dimly, too, she comprehended the reason she had been brought with them; or thought she did.

'Quite a shock to you all, I see,' said Crayshaw. 'You really are nothing like as good as you think you are, Hammond, nothing like as good. I intended tonight to deal with all of you, if you did oblige me by coming. I have an aeroplane waiting, in which Hershall and Craigie will travel to the Continent, and on the Continent they will be well cared for, believe me.'

Hammond snapped: 'You won't get away with it!'

'My dear fellow,' crowed Crayshaw, 'of course I shall get away with it. I have a number of forceful young men here. Until you arrived they were in the cellars, but now they are spreading about the house, some of them even going outside, to make quite sure that you don't get away.'

He paused, and the door opened.

Hammond remembered from Audeley Street how well Crayshaw's pauses were judged, and he was not surprised to see the man who entered was carrying a tommy-gun at the ready.

Marion's teeth clamped together.

'I don't *want* to be violent,' murmured Crayshaw, 'but I do want to make sure that you all realise the impossibility of escape. A pity really—for you, I mean—that you interfered!'

Hammond said harshly: 'We haven't stopped interfering yet.'

'You have very nearly done so,' Crayshaw assured him. 'One burst from the machine gun will silence all of you for ever. If I were you, gentlemen, I should take your hands from your pockets and drop your guns.'

Hammond said: 'All in good time. Did you know that the house was surrounded, that the grounds were packed with police and Home Guard as well as my men? Or did you think that the body from the car really deceived us?'

Crayshaw halted in the middle of a step, and stared towards him. Marion knew that Hammond and the others had stopped bluffing; they had got what they wanted, but she could not understand just what it was.

Crayshaw shouted: 'That is a lie!'

'No, no,' said Hammond testily. 'We haven't time to spend in lying. When you "died", Crayshaw, you expected us to come here, of course. You knew we would want to look round, but you thought that being convinced that you were dead we would take no particular precautions. Instead, we took a lot. We didn't believe you were dead, my dear chap.'

Crayshaw drew a deep breath, half-turned towards the man with the tommy-gun, who was staring towards him. Mike Errol took an automatic from his pocket so slowly and nonchalantly that he might have been drawing out a cigarette-case. The moment was so perfectly chosen that neither Crayshaw nor his henchman knew what was happening until the sneeze of the silenced automatic sighed through the room. The bullet took the man holding the tommy-gun in the shoulder. He spun sideways, and Mark Errol, nearer than Mike, moved towards him with such speed that he had the tommy-gun before it reached the floor.

'Surprise and effect,' murmured Hammond. 'Crayshaw, you

have the unmistakable defects of your race. Excellent planners all, but so lacking in imagination. I'm almost disappointed in you.'

Crayshaw shouted: 'You are mad, you are crazy! Everyone knows that Sir Noel Crayshaw is an Englishman!' He was completely unprepared for failure, so sure, so very sure that everything would work out as he had planned.

Hammond said amusedly: 'Oh yes, everyone knows that. But then, you see, you're not Sir Noel Crayshaw.'

## 22

# THE TRUTH ABOUT CRAYSHAW

Only Marion made an exclamation of astonishment.
'You—you are mad!' The voice rose upwards. 'I am
Crayshaw, I am—'

Hammond said wearily, 'Oh, don't be a fool. You
think Hershall is here. You're supposed to be a lifelong
friend of Hershall's but you don't recognise an understudy
when you see one.'

Crayshaw gasped: '*What?* What is that?'

'I think you heard,' said Hammond. 'Lord, the mistakes
you've made in this show! But I've suspected the truth about
you for a long time, from the moment you acted differently
from the way Hilary expected. You didn't think of that, did
you? You knew the story of the cross, you even arranged for
her to lose it so that it would explain her "suicide" at my flat.
Your first mistake was to stage it there and not in Ferdinand's.
You thought you would confuse the issue, you thought you
would draw the fire to Ferdinand and Fryer, that you would
be all right yourself. That was mistake number two. I
suspected the calm way you received Hilary, when she

expected you to be so ramping mad she was almost afraid of her life. Do you follow the error in psychology, Crayshaw, the typical German error?'

'Crayshaw' licked his lips.

'By making another attempt on Hilary's life you told me one thing quite clearly. *You didn't want Hilary to see you again.* It took me about five minutes to find a reason: because she would recognise you. Ferdinand was killed because he was in love with Hilary, and because he too could give you away.

'You kidnapped the real Crayshaw,' Hammond went on, 'and took his place. Officially you were immersed in business, actually you were keeping out of the limelight. You had your three colleagues—the only men, excepting Hershall, who knew you really well—murdered, and Hershall himself you avoided, getting in touch with him only through the telephone. You planned to get the conference staged here, which is why Cavendish's place was burned down, and you hoped with the help of your own Home Guard unit to get Hershall and perhaps several others safely away. But once we had the letter, you knew that we would be warned about the twenty-first, which is tomorrow, so you changed the day. I asked the Prime Minister to alter nothing, solely to keep you confused, and you swallowed the bait whole, assuming that no one—except perhaps me—had any idea what you were planning.'

'Crayshaw' was breathing so hard that he appeared to be struggling for breath, as Hammond continued: 'There was just the possibility that I was wrong, and so we arranged to have Fenn sent, instead of Hershall. Then we followed up, and you said your little piece. It was easy, wasn't it? He paused for a moment, and then went on more quickly: 'It was clever, too, up to a point, even the killing of the real Crayshaw, whose body was thrown out of the car this evening. You thought that once Hershall and Craigie had gone out of the country, you could continue to impersonate Crayshaw, even to the point of attending the conference, which would have to be held eventually. You could then get information of vast importance and pass it on. There was little chance of detection, for Crayshaw's circle of intimate friends numbered only three, and these you had killed.'

The man who had called himself Crayshaw seemed to have shrivelled. He backed slowly to a chair, peering at Hammond through eyes which were filled with dread.

Loftus said: 'He's finished, Bruce, it's over.'

'Crayshaw' muttered: 'It's over, it's all over.' He shivered, and then raised his voice. 'You have defeated me, Hammond. I did not know that you were so near to the truth. I did not know.' He raised a hand and dropped it, raised it again and put it to his waistcoat pocket. The fingers, fiddling there, came out with a cigar case. He extracted a cigar, groped again for a match. 'You are right on every count, Hammond. Thanks to the accursed refugee you learned of the date.' He struck a match, letting it burn slowly in his fingers. 'It was so well arranged,' he went on tonelessly, 'every detail prepared. It was a blow when you took Fryer and closed the Lamplighter. I had hoped to keep you occupied with Fryer, he was there to draw the attention from me, he was—'

'Crayshaw' put the cigar to his lips again, then suddenly threw it from him.

Hammond saw it hit the ground, saw also the wisp of vapour which came from it. The Errols swung their guns round, but 'Crayshaw' dropped to knee level. As he went down, he took a small gun from his pocket and fired at Mark Errol.

Mark took the bullet in his shoulder.

All were now coughing helplessly.

'Crayshaw' reached the hall.

He went to the front door, pulled it open, and snapped:

'Get away from here, tell everyone to get away!'

There were men of his bodyguard, men of whom he had boasted, within hearing distance; but Davidson was there too. Davidson sent a high-pitched 'hallo!' echoing about the grounds, telling the waiting men to expect trouble, then he himself slipped into the Grange.

He saw Hammond half-way across the hall, coughing violently, and he saw the man he thought was Crayshaw at the head of the stairs.

'After—him,' croaked Hammond. 'Get—Craigie.'

Davidson leapt after the bearded man. Hammond followed, more slowly. He was less affected than Loftus or Marion, having moved to the door more quickly; his aim now was to save Gordon Craigie.

He reached the first landing, as Davidson streaked up the second flight of stairs.

Then he heard a shot.

He reached the top landing and saw Davidson reeling against the wall, one hand at his shoulder, his gun dangling uselessly.

Hammond went on.

He reached Craigie's door as the man left to guard him came out. Two shots were fired almost at the same time. Hammond felt the wind of a bullet past his cheek, and saw the man fall.

He pushed the door open.

Fenn still slept, Craigie standing beside him, as the bearded man raised his gun.

Hammond fired, and 'Crayshaw's' gun clattered to the floor. He spun round, his eyes glaring. Hammond covered him, still coughing, unable to find words.

The man who had played so long and desperate a game

stood quite still, helpless and completely beaten, robbed of every prize he had hoped to win. He swayed for a few seconds, very slowly, his left hand groped towards his pocket, stopped there, and then fell to his side.

Hammond said, 'It's really over this time.'

'Crayshaw' croaked: 'If the refugee hadn't arrived, if—'

There was a moment of silence, and then Hammond said very slowly: 'Tell me, before you go right out. Did you know Marion Caroll before you started this?'

As he spoke, Marion reached the door.


There was a long silence in that room.

Craigie saw Marion, but made no sign. Hammond had no idea that she was behind him. Crayshaw's eyes were closed, and he leaned against a chair; it seemed likely that he would collapse before he could speak.

Then: 'Curse you,' he muttered. 'God curse your soul!'

Hammond said: 'Answer that one question, will you?' He stepped to the dying man's side, leaned over him. Marion, watching, motionless, as if at a scene enacted a long way off, knew that it was the one thought in his mind. He wanted to know, he had to know. The streak of ruthlessness in the man had never been more apparent; he was not interested in 'Crayshaw's' dying, or his pain. He had no more feeling for the bearded man than he had had for Fryer or Esteven. The one question burned in his mind, to the exclusion of everything else.

'Crayshaw', sitting in a chair and gasping for breath, opened his eyes and looked into Hammond's.

'No,' he said. 'She wasn't—with me.'

Hammond straightened up. Then he bent over the man again, in an effort to make him more comfortable.

Marion looked past him towards Craigie.

Craigie shook his head. She saw it, hesitated, and then understood. She moved from the doorway and out of sight. She went blindly down the stairs, and as she did so she heard the shouting and the shooting from the grounds.

She knew vaguely that Hammond's men were having what they probably considered a good time. She knew that the men 'Crayshaw' had gathered about him were helplessly outnumbered, that it was unlikely any of them would get through.

She recalled, in a vague, distant fashion, everything that had happened. She remembered the ruthless application with which Hammond had treated everything that had happened, from the clearing up of the fifth column squad in the Home Guard. She realised with a vivid clarity the fact that Hammond had seen through the side issues utterly and completely. He had conceived the motive for the organisation, he had been proved right not once but a dozen times.

He had let nothing influence him; and he had suspected her. Acting as if she was in his complete confidence, he had kept her close to him so that he could watch her. The hurt was a physical pain, something she could not bear, that struck so deeply that she was detached from all that was going on about her.

Through the open door she saw flashes of light, occasionally the beam of a torch-light, and frequently she heard shooting.

She walked unsteadily down the stairs and reached the porch. Not until she stepped into it did she know that two men were standing there. Nor did they at first see her.

'By George, Loftus, your fellows are having the time of their lives!' one of them said.

The other one answered: 'The odds are too easy, sir.' He

paused. 'Lord, you gave me a shock when you came up the drive.'

Hershall chuckled.

'I gave myself a shock, I can tell you. Had an idea that it might not be Crayshaw, and thought I'd better see what you and Hammond were up to. When I turned into the drive, this shindy began. Well, I don't think there's much more to worry about. An odd business. Queer fellow, Hammond.'

Loftus said: 'Yes and no, sir. He—'

Loftus stopped abruptly, seeing Marion appear. Her expression was enough to make him, look at her in astonishment, while Hershall glanced at her casually enough, and then with greater attention.

Hershall took her arm, guiding her into the sitting room.

'We'd better get inside, my dear,' he said. 'There may be a stray bullet.'

Abruptly she turned to Loftus: 'Bill, how long has he suspected me?'

Loftus drew a deep breath and then, bracing himself, said quietly: 'In the first place, Marion, it was I who suspected you. I wondered how the news about the boots leaked out, and wasn't sure that Brice was the real explanation. I suggested that Bruce watched you carefully. He called me a fool, had you transferred from Emile to Hilary, from Hilary to himself.' Loftus paused. 'How did you know?'

'He was asking Crayshaw,' Marion said in a low voice.

As she spoke, Hammond entered the room. He went straight to her, and put an arm about her shoulders. 'I had to know,' he said gruffly. 'I couldn't let there be even a shadow of doubt. I told Loftus that he was talking through the back of his neck, but—'

Hershall gave a little cough.

Marion said: 'It doesn't matter, Bruce, it doesn't matter.'

'It matters a lot,' said Hammond quietly. 'I could have had you left with Emile, you know, or even Hilary, and could have made sure that you were watched—by someone else, I mean.'

He was looking at her, and she could not evade his gaze. 'I wanted to watch you myself. I still do, I always shall. I wanted you around, Marion, I even made excuses for taking you to the Lamplighter, I even took it quite for granted that you'd come here tonight.'

She felt a weight lifting from her heart.

'Is that the whole truth, Bruce?'

'The whole of it,' he assured her.

Hershall gave a second louder, more assertive cough. He beamed on Marion, then turned with obvious relief to Hammond. 'Well, well, now that that little matter is settled to at least two people's satisfaction, I want to hear how you pulled the Crayshaw business off.'

Hammond said, almost shyly: 'Oh, once the pieces began to fall into place, it was easy enough. The great thing is that Craigie's all right. He's actually started a search of the house!' Hammond chuckled. 'When he knows that you're here he'll get a shock.'

'You didn't seem particularly surprised,' said Hershall.

Hammond looked at him amusedly.

'I wasn't,' he said. 'I knew quite well that if I told you what I thought, you'd want to do something about it yourself, and—' he shrugged.

Hershall eyed Hammond curiously, then gave a deep laugh.

'Yes—es. I'm not sure that I envy you, Miss Caroll, he's an unpredictable young man.' He took out his cheroot case. 'We may as well stay here the night, I suppose?' he asked with the relish of a small boy.

'The service will be a bit of a problem,' said Hammond.

'Oh, we'll manage. I've no intention of going to sleep, anyhow. Fetch Craigie, and let's talk the whole thing over.'

By the following day the fact was established that the real Crayshaw had been kidnapped and that a certain Baron von Linth, educated at Oxford and resident for some time in England before the war, had essayed the great gamble. By then, too, Emile was assured that he had nothing more to worry about and that thanks to him a Nazi plot had been uncovered. Hilary Crayshaw, in the nursing-home and much improved, learned of the truth and did not appear surprised.

Hammond wondered what would happen to her eventually; he heard a few months afterwards that her cure had been successful and that she had joined the W.A.A.F. It pleased him.

Before then, at Crayshaw Grange, was found a supply of the poison used on the arrows. One by one the men who had helped 'Crayshaw' were rounded up. Hammond and Loftus admitted not only the thoroughness of the organisation but the amazing ingenuity of its methods of attack.

At Hammond's flat, the following evening, Loftus said as much.

'The whole plot might have succeeded but for Bruce's damned obstinacy.'

'I was running round in circles half the time,' Hammond protested. 'It just worked out my way.' He yawned then lit a cigarette. Examining it, he said slowly: 'Are you going back to the nursing-home for a few days, Bill?'

'I'd thought of it.'

'We'll join you, and make it a six-some,' said Hammond. 'Is that all right with you, Marion?'

'We'll be there,' said Marion.

# ABOUT THE AUTHOR

John Creasey, born in 1908, was a paramount English crime and science fiction writer who used myriad pseudonyms for more than six hundred novels. He founded the UK Crime Writers' Association in 1953. In 1962, his book *Gideon's Fire* received the Edgar Award for Best Novel from the Mystery Writers of America. Many of the characters featured in Creasey's titles became popular, including George Gideon of Scotland Yard, who was the basis for a subsequent television series and film. Creasey died in Salisbury, UK, in 1973.

# DEPARTMENT Z

FROM OPEN ROAD MEDIA

OPEN ROAD

INTEGRATED MEDIA

OPEN ROAD
INTEGRATED MEDIA

www.ingramcontent.com/pod-product-compliance
Lightning Source LLC
Chambersburg PA
CBHW020554020726
47494CB00006B/2063